T0198615

City of Syn

Gateway to Erotica

Nicole Cade

iUniverse, Inc.
New York   Bloomington

City of Syn
Gateway to Erotica

iUniverse books may be ordered through booksellers or by contacting:

iUniverse
1663 Liberty Drive
Bloomington, IN 47403
www.iuniverse.com
1-800-Authors (1-800-288-4677)

ISBN: 978-1-4401-8030-9 (sc)
ISBN: 978-1-4401-8031-6 (ebk)

Printed in the United States of America

iUniverse rev. date: 10/23/2009

To the boys of my past, the man of my future, and the city beautiful for being such a fabulous playground.

Introduction

"It is a fool whose addiction is to the butterflies."

In every romance, every flirtatious friendship, and every lustful one-night stand, we look for it. For some, it's the butterflies; for others it's an OMG moment; and for a hopeful few, it's the gentle swell of the heart. These moments we look for, that we dream of, that we wish for, are when lightning strikes.

It's the initial moment when you know you have to have more, that you can't breathe and all you can do is feel, your every thought consumed by pure desire. This moment comes once to a relationship, however long it is. Lightning never strikes the same place twice, and so we keep searching, trying to duplicate that moment, to prolong the bliss and the searing intensity of that desire.

The following stories were written about those moments. This isn't your mother's erotica, with flowering romance dotted with forbidden kisses in moonlit gardens. The scenes played out in this collection offer a variety, the something-for-everyone approach. If you like it soft and slow, "Key West" would be the story for you. If you're in

3

for something a little wilder, "Truth or Dare" might do the trick. Or if you're looking to indulge in pure fantasy, "Sexcraft" will surely get your attention.

No matter what the story, the scene, or the people involved, each offers its own unique take on the moment that lightning strikes.

Mountain Retreat

The rain was coming down faster; the lights flickered every so often. She knew the power wouldn't stay on much longer, and she wished he were there already. She was worried about the roads; they got very slippery during storms. He had called an hour ago and said he was on his way from the airport, but that was almost two hours ago.

They had been looking forward to this weekend for ages. When she was finally able to secure the house for the weekend, she was ecstatic and couldn't wait to share her mountain retreat with him. Now, as the storm grew stronger, she couldn't wait to feel his strong arms around her and taste his hungry mouth on hers. The more she thought about it, the more she got turned on. Her body was slowly becoming a mass of tingling sensations partly due to the energy of the lightning flashing outside and partly because they hadn't been together in three weeks. The anticipation was killing her.

They'd been together for almost six months, and since the beginning, the sex had been amazing. He was as intellectually stimulating as he was sexually exciting. Since she had been in Denver this previous week on business, they had arranged for him to fly up for this little tryst, and she had decided to "set the mood." Not that they really needed any setting—they were ravenous for each other. She lit about three dozen candles throughout the house, beginning in the living room, then leading up the stairs to the loft and all around the master bedroom.

Darkness soon fell over the house, and she could no longer see the road. But she could clearly see her reflection in the floor-to-ceiling windows. She had dressed to kill; her long dark hair was wild and floated down her shoulders to her waist. The dress was one of her own creations, a soft black velvet affair with indigo accents, a medieval style with fingertip-length bell sleeves and a tight bodice that left no room to hide her voluptuous breasts. She was wearing nothing underneath save for the thigh-high suede boots she knew he loved. Oh yes, he'd be pleased.

Finally, she saw a figure approaching the house. Her heart started to beat faster as she watched his tall, confident stride. So much power and strength in such a simple movement. Her limbs started to tremble as he grew closer. She moved away from the window to lie on the chaise and then changed her mind. Why draw this out any longer? She was already getting those familiar streaks of pleasure in her lower abdomen. So she met him at the door.

As soon as the door swung open, his arms were around her. He felt so wonderful and warm, encompassing her in a definitive male aroma. He buried his face in her neck and her hair, inhaling deeply and relishing her sweet, musky scent. His hands twined up in her silky tresses. He pulled her head back, and without a word, he brought his lips down on hers. It was a crushing, hungry kiss, a kiss of possession.

His tongue pried her lips open; slashing his mouth against hers, he invaded the small, sweet cavern, their tongues dancing in a rhythm known only to lovers. Her hands around his neck kept him close. He gentled the kiss, nibbling her lips and trailing down to her neck and shoulders. He stepped back a moment and looked into her luminous green eyes. Taking note of her swollen lips and trembling hands, his eyes moved downward to take in the soft, milky white flesh heaving at the top of her gown. He continued to stroke her as he swallowed the vision standing before him.

His hands moved to her waist, pulling her back to him. He could feel the sweet throbbing in his groin as her warm body fit into his. They stood there, a moment in time, gazing into each other's soul—knowing, wanting, and needing the hot, intense passion they both knew was bubbling between them.

Lightning flashed as she took his hand and led him to the sofa. She gently pushed him down and knelt between his legs. Pushing his long sable hair back over his shoulders, she started unbuttoning his shirt, running her hands over his warm chest. She nuzzled her face in his neck, savoring the feeling of his hot skin. His hands resting on her thighs began to stir; she stopped and put her small hands on top to quiet him. It was difficult to be so restrained when all she could think of was tearing his clothes off and fucking him senseless right here on the couch. She could feel his hardness on the inside of her thigh, growing hotter as she continued her seductive ministrations.

He didn't say a word as her hands worked his shirt off. She slid down to the floor, giving him a teasing view of her décolletage. She worked her nimble fingers to slide his pants off and simultaneously slip him out of his underwear. She guided her lips to his throbbing flesh and circled her tongue around his head, teasing him. She felt him tense under her touch, his hands pulling gently at her hair. She continued her onslaught on his manhood, taking him completely inside her mouth and back out again, moving her tongue and her lips in a rhythmic pattern.

He watched her head moving below his waist, her hair glinting in the candlelight and brushing his thighs as she continued her intimate caresses. He brushed her hair to the side so he could see her tiny pink tongue darting in and out and around his hard cock. He watched her soft red lips swallow every aching inch of him. He knew the end was near and wanted to stop her, but he couldn't find

the strength to end the spell she was working on him. She shifted upward slightly so her breasts were pressed exquisitely against the base of his member. She began to pick up speed, fucking him with her cherry lips.

He felt the end nearing and quickly twisted his hands up in her hair and pulled her head back. Looking into his eyes, she smiled mischievously. He pulled her to her feet and turned her around. He ran his fingers down her back and undid the cording that held her bodice so tight. Sliding his hands to the front, he pulled her into his lap. Hungrily, he slipped inside her gown and caressed the twin mounds that had beckoned so deliciously only moments before. He gently rolled her raspberry nipples between his fingers until they were stiff with wanting. She arched her back into him, resting her head on his shoulder. Her hands gently grazed the outside of his thighs as he teased and taunted her breasts.

He slid a hand between her legs, parting them. Slowly he pulled up the skirt of her dress, nestling himself against her moist pink flesh. She could feel his hard cock against her and rocked slightly, teasing him. He turned his head toward hers and sought out her kiss while his fingers parted her tender flesh down below. Finding the small slit, he slipped two fingers inside, and she let out a small gasp at the welcome invasion. He squeezed her breast and deepened his kiss as he plied her wet pussy with his fingers, pinpointing the spot he knew would make her come.

She began to stir against him, moving lightly against his maleness. She wanted him, needed him. She ground her round bottom down into his lap as his fingers moved deeper inside her. He abandoned her breasts and positioned her legs on the outside of his thighs. She moved her arms up and pulled his head back down toward hers, devouring his lips, desperately searching for something. His expert hands worked her into frenzy; he was holding her to him, yet she couldn't seem to be still. One hand pushed deeper into her while the other toyed with her clit, bringing her to a fevered pitch. Their kiss deepened, and she clung tightly to him, her breathing shallow as she grew closer. She moaned deep in her throat, arching fiercely against his chest.

His hands came to an abrupt stop and she breathed a panicked no into his neck.

"Please, oh god, please don't stop," she said.

Slowly, he withdrew his other hand and brought it up to her mouth. He gently nudged one finger into her mouth, toying with her tongue. She tasted the sweet juice on him, and it only stoked the fire more intensely. In a swift motion, he gathered her in his arms and began walking toward the stairs. Her eyes were half closed as she recovered from the near ecstasy of the previous moment.

Once inside the bedroom, he placed her on weak limbs and took her face in his hands. Kissing her softly, he lightly brushed his hands over her hair. She brought her

hands to his shoulders, squeezing him closer to her. She was shivering, and he was so warm. He sensed her chill, but instead of pulling her tighter, he stepped back and slid her gown down her shoulders, till it pooled at her feet. She was left with nothing but the soft suede of her boots keeping the chill off her trembling legs. Her long hair swirled down her back and over her shoulders, nipping at her candlelit breasts.

He pulled the covers off the mammoth four-poster bed and led her to it. She sat down on the edge of the bed and let him remove her shoes, his hands caressing her as he slid the soft fabric down to her slender ankles. He placed his hand behind her and laid her down on the mound of pillows, covering her shivering body with his own heat. She felt his hardness nestle in the junction of her thighs and arched slightly, pushing her breasts upward and crushing them against the hard wall of his chest. He brought his lips to the hollow of her neck, caressing her with his tongue and the soft sweetness of his lips. She allowed a lilting moan to escape, and his arms went around her tightly.

He trailed his kisses down her neck to tease the taut nipples. His tongue made white-hot streaks around her aching breasts; the more he licked and sucked and teased, the higher she arched into him. She wanted him to devour her, and she was just as ravenous for him. He extended his blazing trail to her abdomen, down her hips, and to the inside of her thighs, stopping to glance up at her. She

13

watched him with her lust-filled jade orbs, and he knew their game of sweet torture had come to an end. It was time to reap the rewards.

He slid his body upward, shifting so his legs were between hers, opening her. She took his face in her hands and kissed him deeply, beginning the dance as old as time. She could feel the tip of his throbbing cock at her wet opening, pushing gently against her. She shifted her body, moving her legs wider apart and inviting his entrance. She looked into the dark pools of his eyes and watched the storm rage as he pushed into her. She cried out as he filled her tender canal. Her fingers dug into his shoulders as he drove into the tight honeyed flesh, savoring the exquisite sensation of being wrapped inside her. He crushed his lips to hers, driving into her mouth and her womanhood again and again. She arched against him, matching his hungry rhythm, taking every inch of him and seeking out more, needing that sweet release she knew was inevitable.

The thunder crashed outside and lightning slashed across their thriving bodies. She screamed his name, and he drove into her harder, faster, bringing her to the point of no return. Her breathing was shallow and her words were incoherent. She grasped at him, letting his body envelop her in a passionate embrace. She felt him burning into her, an indelible imprint left behind each time. She seared his cock with her slick, sweet wetness as he pushed inside the tight opening. She sheathed him, a perfect fit.

He surged within her once more before she buried her face in his shoulder and screamed his name one last time. He could feel her honeyed juices as she came all over him. At once, his pulsing cock thrust deep inside her, and he let his own juices rage through the trembling body beneath him.

He looked down into her face, flushed with the passion that still bubbled beneath the surface and kissed her softly. She entangled her fingers in his long hair and pulled him closer. Desperately, he wanted to collapse upon her, but instead he rolled slightly to the side of her, cradling her in his arms. She curved her body into his, stretching like a lazy kitten beside him. Their breathing was still ragged and shallow as they lay still, gazing at the storm that continued to swirl outside their sweet retreat.

Insatiable

As he pulled into the driveway, he noticed no lights on in the house. Yet her car was in the garage, so he knew she was home. He hoped she was still awake—but if she wasn't, he would just have to wake her up, he thought with a mischievous grin.

He pulled the handle of the door and was immediately greeted by the muted sounds of Type O Negative wafting from down the hall. He knew by the music what her mood was and said a silent thank you, for he was after the very same thing. Her. He took off his leather jacket, boots, and shirt, leaving only the black jeans he'd worn to work. He ran his hands through his dark hair and started off toward the music and the little wanton angel he knew was waiting for him.

The sight that greeted him stunned him for a moment and sent white-hot bolts searing through his pelvis. She was lying in the middle of the bed, completely stripped of clothing, with the navy blue satin sheets twisted around her. Two candles flickered on either side of her head, the firelight bouncing off her writhing body. Her long, curly hair was a tangled web of blue-black ribbons on the pillows.

The vision of her lithe body held him captive for a moment. He watched her back arch as she ran her hands over her ample chest, cupping her breasts; she let out a small whimper when she pinched her taut nipples. One hand left her breast to continue its voyage over her pale abdomen to the smooth mound at the junction of her thighs. He watched in throbbing amazement as she parted her legs to reveal her swollen pink flesh.

She must have been at this for a little while because she was already nearing her peak, and he'd only been watching a few moments. He silently removed his jeans and boxers, his eyes never leaving her. Her head was moving from side to side, and she was arching up higher as she toyed with her clit. She let an occasional moan escape every now and then, completely oblivious that he was watching her. He stood over her at the bottom of the bed, his cock standing at attention and waiting patiently for its sweet reward. He knelt at the foot of the bed, and her head snapped up, her eyes round with surprise at his quiet entry.

He took the hand that still rested on her wet opening and slid her fingers into his mouth. He tasted her, licking every inch of her fingers, suddenly starving to taste more of her. He shoved her thighs wide apart and plunged his tongue inside her. She let out a cry at the surprise invasion.

His hands grabbed her ass, kneading her with his fingers and bringing her up closer to him. Her hands were running through his hair, pushing him into her. His tongue swept over her most intimate parts, sending lightning through her body as her pink lips swelled and signaled her release.

He felt her whole body begin to quicken, so he used his thumbs to spread her lips even wider, lapping up the sweetness that flowed from her depths. He glanced up at her face and saw her looking at him, passion simmering in the emerald depths of her eyes.

"Come for me, honey. Come for me now," he said, and he pushed his tongue back inside her.

At his command, she felt the wave rise within her, and when she felt his tongue pushing into her, she tossed her head back, her hair spilling over the bed like water, and let the waves wash over her, repeating his name again and again. He continued his oral ministrations as the tide within her ebbed.

She lay back on the pillows and felt him kneel between her legs. She glanced up at him, noticing his wicked smile and the way his hair fell over one eye. He tossed his head back and put his hands on her waist, lifting her up out of the mound of pillows. When she was before him, he slowly turned her around. Sweeping her long hair to the side, he brought his lips to her neck and his hands to her swollen breasts, massaging them with the tips of his fingers. She sighed, rubbing her ass against the swollen cock behind her. He placed his hand on her belly to hold her, groaning at her softness pressed tightly against his hard member. Not willing to wait any longer, he pushed her onto her hands in front of him, then leaned over her and pushed his cock to the tight, wet opening of her pussy. He wrapped his hand in her hair, gently but forcefully pulling her head back. He whispered in her ear, "Are you ready for me?" She nodded slightly, and he pushed into her without another word.

Even though she knew it was coming, she still let out a startled cry at the sudden fullness inside her. Her cry gave him a sense of satisfaction. After watching her play with herself, he could think of nothing else but fucking her. He pushed deeper into her, then moving upright and letting her hair go, he placed his hands on her hips and watched as the tight pink flesh stretched around him. He continued pumping her, noticing his cock was shiny with her juices.

She could feel his heavy sacs hitting against her swollen clit as he pounded her, creating a double onslaught to her already dripping pussy. He leaned over her again, deeply embedding himself inside her. She turned her head toward him. In the unusual stillness, she could feel him throbbing, and she tightened her muscles around him, tempting him. He gasped at the sudden contraction and pushed deeper.

"I want more," he whispered, and then slowly began pumping in and out while still leaning over her. He slowly came to a stop and pulled out, leaving her tight woman

flesh wet and swollen, begging for another release. He turned her back around and kissed her hard on the mouth, crushing her body to his.

She brought her hands to his ass and pulled his groin to her silky skin, feeling the mix of sweat and sex on his skin. In one swift movement, he pulled her legs out from under them and was on top of her. His body fit snugly between her legs. He parted them wider and pushed her ankles up over his shoulders, and still with his tongue buried in her mouth, he buried his cock deep in her taut pink canal. She arched against him and moaned against his mouth. She rocked back and forth as he plunged in and out of her. Wrapped tight in his arms, her body racked with pleasure, she felt his pace increase as he slammed into her body.

His control was slipping; he wanted to feel her come one more time before he filled her completely. He let out a low growl against her lips and tore himself away to look into her stormy jade eyes.

"Now, honey, please now," he pleaded.

She shifted slightly and increased the friction on her clit, bringing her moments away from a mind-blowing orgasm. He felt her tighten around him and push her breasts against his sweaty chest. She clawed at his back and screamed as he ground his thick cock into her again and again. He brought his mouth down to hers in another crushing kiss and let himself fill her, crying out her name and searing her with his white-hot cum.

His breathing ragged and uneven, he gentled the kiss, slowing his animal-like movements. He cradled her in his arms, feeling her still throbbing around him. She laid her flushed cheek against his shoulder and sighed, enjoying the still pleasurable sensation of him inside her. The slept in this lover's embrace as the candles played across their sweaty bodies, only to wake and begin the ritual again.

It's 1:00 AM, and the dream came again. Only this time I went with it. I was there with him. Still, I couldn't place where we were. It was nearly dark, with only a little light, but I didn't know where the light was coming from.

I was trembling, holding him tightly as his lips moved over my skin. I responded to him with such heat and intensity, I can still feel the longing. I pulled at him, begging for more. My inexperienced pleas fell on deaf ears as he had his own agenda for my acquiescent body. How could I deny him? This was what I wanted, wasn't it?

Every time his lips left me, I wanted to cry in disappointment. His touch was like none of the others. It was so sure, yet it was soft. I knew he was experienced.

In the dream, there was always a sense of the forbidden. It was always this thought that stirred my first desires.

I'm lying in bed, my body a mass of unfulfilled wanting. The feeling is so consuming it becomes an ache I need to quell. I close my eyes again, seeing the dark shadow of his body as he moves further down my length, kissing me in places that have never known such intimate touches.

While my dream plays in my head, I trace my fingers over my moist skin. I slide them over my neck, feeling my rapid heartbeat in the sensitive hollow above my chest. Imagining his hands molding my flesh to his, I run my palms over the tops of my breasts, feeling my hard nipples waiting for his elusive kiss. I pinch them gently. The throbbing nub between my legs quakes at my touch. I groan, knowing I cannot stop this fantasy.

Always in my dream, he would kiss and lick at my breasts for what seemed like ages, leaving my innocence wet and begging for release. But as much as I desire him and my body begs to be taken, I am afraid. It is my fear of his impending entrance that wakes me from the astral lovemaking.

However, not afraid of my own touch, I slip one hand between my parted thighs and gently separate my puffy lips. Finally touching my hot sex is such a relief that I moan loudly. Turning my head to glance at my still sleeping roommate, I am relieved to see she has not stirred.

I sink deeper into the dream, toying with my nipples while easing my fingers into the sweet lava that is seeping from within. I'm deliberately teasing myself, wanting to draw the dream out as long as I can. I want so desperately to come, but I go slowly. I purposely build delightful sensations on top of one another so when I do reach my peak, I will crash hard for a seemingly endless amount of time.

Dipping my fingers into my own wetness, I squirm under the covers—it is his lips now between my legs, his tongue seeking out my clit, teasing my beckoning opening. I'm moaning and sighing now. I'm lost in the dream, in his touch, his intimate kiss. I want to grab his head and pull him deeper into me. The teasing, taunting flicks of his tongue on my most secret places are agonizing. Never complete, again and again I am left crying out for more. Finally I let my finger slip fully inside my virgin flesh under the guise of the dream. I've never experienced a more sensual feeling.

My eyes squeeze tight as I will my subconscious to continue my dream. I am spiraling, my virgin body not used to the hot intensity of the soft caresses. Pushing my finger in and out, I begin a continuous massage of my swollen clit.

My dream threatens to overtake my reality as the images flashing in my head are intensified by my physical response. It is a vicious cycle. The deeper I get into the dream, the more intense my response is, and the greater my response, the deeper I sink into the dream. I cannot see his face, only feel him. I push harder, his tongue insistent. I squeeze my breasts, his hand rough. I tease my clit, his lips hot. I am climbing, faster now, reaching an unknown height. I feel like my body is searching for something, only I don't know what.

I know my sheets no longer cover me. My legs are spread wide to allow his mouth better access. Deeper inside I push, quickening the pressure on my clit. His ministrations are nonstop and I am lost, a nonentity only left to accept what is done to me. I know I am almost there, the search about to end. I am anxious to know what awaits me, yet I do not want this sexual journey to end.

My dream dictates my reality. All of a sudden I am filled with his tongue, the pressure on my clit almost unbearable, my nipples on fire to his touch. I am unraveling. My body lifts to meet him, and like an avalanche I am devoured. My soul is buried in inexplicable throbbing, my womb quivers, my muscles shake, and my mind is pulsing. I know I must have screamed. No one could keep that phenomenal feeling inside. The sensations go on and on, my body soaking in sweat, juice running between my legs onto the sheets. I still writhe against the subconscious caresses. I had reached the top and am now sliding down the other side.

The images in my mind begin to fade. I am sad to let him go. There is a sense about his departure though: I know he will be back.

The Hotel

The intensity of this night had been building for months. Their casual Internet friendship was building to something she'd not known before. She was terrified of what was going to happen tonight. She was conflicted between the ice queen side of her that never let emotions take control and the writer in her who was unwilling to give up the experience out of fear. She had to remember he was nothing to her, merely a plaything to facilitate yet another adventure into the erotic playgrounds she frequented.

Try as she might, though, every time they talked, the sweet dulcet tones of his voice entered her mind and she could not shake the tingle he left her with. They had met right after Halloween, sharing stories of their Samhain experiences. There was something about him she just couldn't place her finger on, but it kept her coming back for more time and time again. He had been pushing to meet since December, but she had been reluctant. Once she decided to go through with it, they weren't able to coordinate their schedules. In the interim, she had heard of a similar experience through a friend and knew she had to make it her own. She smiled fondly, remembering when she first told him about it. He was shocked at her quick turnaround and boldness but nevertheless agreed immediately. He understood her drive and her needs; his was not a matter of emotion, and for that she was grateful.

Finally, things seemed to fall into place. She had an unexpected trip to Chicago, and they agreed this was the perfect opportunity. So she booked a room at her favorite downtown hotel and e-mailed him the time and place. He wrote her back with a great big smiley face. Due to previous plans and other arrangements, they weren't able to talk much during the week prior to their rendezvous, which only increased her excitement. This was so foreign, so not like her. She had only discussed this with her sister and best friend, and they both thought she was nuts. Maybe she was, but she was confident this was something she had to do. Sex, blind, with a virtual stranger ... who would have thought? They had only briefly discussed the possibility of seeing each other after this, but they came to no decision and decided to leave it alone for now.

He didn't know how he tripped into this, but he was certainly happy about it. He'd never done anything like this, much less even entertained the idea. She was constantly surprising him, and this little turn of events blew his mind. For months, he'd wanted to meet with her, but he was patient, knowing she needed time. When she suggested this idea, he was rendered speechless for a moment, wondering where out of left field this came from. But he quickly recovered and agreed, not really thinking she'd go through with it. Then she called to tell him she was in Chicago and would like to put their plan in motion. He scrambled to clear his schedule for the night and next day just in case. He knew she was a no-strings-attached kind of girl, but too much time had passed, and he knew too much for this to be just one lustful night. He also knew he was being used as a guinea pig for her writing, but he honestly didn't care. If the worst thing he did in life was go down in history as a prop in one of her stories, he'd be doing pretty well.

The only time he heard from her that week was an e-mail giving him the location and time. He repeatedly tried to guess what he might expect from this. How different would that soft, sensual voice sound when it was right next to him? Would he crave to see her face even as he touched her body? He couldn't wait and prayed she didn't back out at the last minute.

It was 7:30—he should be calling her any minute. She had already checked into the room and took care to block out all the light from the street with heavy black poster board. She even unplugged the alarm clock to prevent the wicked green light from ruining their fun. With the lights off, she could see nothing but the thin slit under the door from the hallway—and she had instructions for him on that. She had thought about this very carefully and was pleased with herself. She hoped he would be the same.

Snapped out of her reverie by the ringing of her cell phone, she noticed how it lit up the room and made the mental note to shut it off before he entered. Seeing his name on her caller ID, her heart skipped a beat.

"Hello?"

"Ready for this?"

She could hear the smile in his voice, and it made her relax a bit. In a breathless whisper, she answered, "Yes I am."

"Good, 'cause I'm on my way up. Are you nervous?"

"A little, aren't you?"

"I was, but now that it's here I'm not, I just can't wait to have you in my arms."

That comment gave an unfamiliar tug at her heart, and she quickly pushed it aside, not wanting to contemplate its meaning.

"One thing I need you to do before I step out of the bathroom is take the towel I left outside and put it at the bottom of the door after you close it."

He laughed a little, realizing how much thought she put into this. For the first time, he wondered if he would live up to this moment. He'd never questioned his skills as a lover, but knowing how much this particular experience

meant to her, he felt a little stab of nerves and quickly pushed it from his thoughts. He was outside her door, and nothing was going to deter him from entering.

"Okay, sweetheart, I'm here and I've got the towel."

The softness in his voice relaxed her a little bit more, and she hung up the phone when she heard the door click open.

She honestly didn't know what to expect next, but she couldn't seem to find her voice to say anything.

Apparently he couldn't either, because the next thing she knew, the door was opening and she was being pulled into a pair of warm, strong arms. Immediately, her sense of touch and smell were heightened, trying to register his presence all at once. He was about a head taller than she, and her cheek rested on the hard wall of his chest. She could smell a slight tangy musk scent on him, but it wasn't unpleasant or overwhelming. She smiled; she liked the way he smelled. Her arms went up around his neck, the tips of her fingers brushing against his short hair. She could feel his hot breath on her as he kissed the top of her head and nuzzled his cheek against her soft silky curls.

She smelled amazing, like warm honey. He held her tightly to him, hardly believing he was finally here with her. He felt her soft fingers caressing the back of his neck, and the sensation sent chills down his spine.

I'm sure that's not the first time that will happen tonight, he thought.

Her hair felt like satin ribbons against his face, and he moved his hands to feel her hair slip through his fingers. She pulled her head back and gently pulled against his neck, bringing his face closer to hers. She could feel his breath on her lips as they came closer, until she registered the touch of his lips on hers. At the moment of contact, his arm tightened around her waist and his hand wound inside her curls, pressing her deeper into their first kiss. Like a wall tumbling down, the dam had broken and passion was unleashed. Their lips tasted each other, melding together, exploring, painting images their eyes could not confirm. She brought her fingers to his face, running them lightly over his cheeks and down his jaw, filling in her mental portrait of him.

They had not moved from the entrance of the room. Lost in the kiss, stopping was not an option. They were both so hungry for the other and couldn't conceive of separating. Gripping his arms with her hands, she held him as she began to step backward toward the center of the room. Already familiar with the layout, she needed him to follow her. He did so willingly.

Upon backing into the bed, he guided her down, his hand behind her head, covering her body with his own. He reluctantly eased out of the kiss, noting her whispered protest against his mouth as his lips left hers.

Gazing into the dark oblivion, he traced his fingers over her face. He mentally sketched out the delicate heart

shape, guiding his fingertips over her closed eyes, feeling the fringe of her long eyelashes, and stroking her soft cheeks. She turned her head to the side, kissing his palm. He moved his thumb over her swollen lips. She opened her mouth teasingly and sucked him gently. His hand cupped her chin, and he brought his mouth down on hers once again. Slipping his tongue between her lips, he taunted her playfully, inciting her to respond. Her fingers grazed lightly down his neck to his wide shoulders and then down his muscular arms.

She grinned inwardly. Having described themselves throughout their conversations over the last months, finally touching the reality was exciting. Sliding her hands over his chest and down the defined abs she knew he worked hard at, she heard his sharp intake of breath when she reached his waist and slipped her hand under his shirt.

He felt her cool hands on his skin and jumped at the contact. He felt like he could kiss her all night long, easily forgetting there was a soft and willing body beneath him. Completely overwhelmed by the touch of her hands on his stomach and her lips on his mouth, his concentration stalled, and he scrambled to regain control. She continued moving her hands over his warm, smooth skin, taking his shirt higher and higher until she began to tug on it, willing him to take it off. He understood her request and moved quickly to appease her, realizing his need to feel her skin as well. He took his shirt off and placed his hands on her shoulders, feeling her body relax against him she rested her cheek on the skin just above his jeans. The simple gesture made him tremble a bit. He stood there a moment, his hands running up and down her arms to her sides. He found the hem of her shirt and pulled it up over her head. Tossing the shirt to the side, he turned back to the bed and reached for her. Finding her not there, he frowned.

She reached out to where she knew he was standing and touched his arm, sliding her hand down till she had his hand in hers. She guided him onto the bed where she reclined with her head resting on the pillows. He positioned himself next to her, anxious and excited. Aching to touch her, the tension was almost tangible. She slid her hand around his neck and pulled him down to her. His body relaxing against her side, they fell into another kiss, more tender this time. Their hunger focused, she savored the taste of his soft lips and sucked the tip of his tongue sweetly. With one hand, he began to explore her exposed skin, lightly trailing a path down her side to her waist and over her hips, and came to what felt like a thin strip of lace. He moved along her thigh, coming to the slow realization that she had greeted him in only a shirt and panties. Now that the shirt was gone, there was only one barrier left. His pulse quickened at his discovery, and his jeans grew tighter.

She held her breath at his gentle touch, arching slightly as a chill coursed over her body. She longed for him to touch her more sensitive parts, but she would not let herself break the spell they held over each other. His fingers made their return journey, stopped at her waist, and he pulled her body toward him, pressing her breasts to his chest. She squirmed against his warmth, needing to get closer, needing to touch all of him. His arms snaked around her back, pulling her deeper into him, mapping her body with his own. He learned every curve, every soft plain, with his body, committing it to memory. She moved her lips down to his jaw, covering him with light kisses along his neck and shoulders, doing her own discovery of the terrain she desperately needed to touch. She could feel his nipples hard against her palms, his stomach taut against her own. She moved her body over him, massaging him with her most sensual parts. She twisted so that now he was lying on his back, his hands restless over her hair, her back, and her shoulders.

Not being able to see where she might go next, he was on edge every moment. With every kiss she pressed into him, he lost more control, slowly giving in to her sweet torture. She took her time, learning him, knowing him, teasing him. She left trails of wet kisses over his chest and stomach, leading down the soft hair that led below his waist. When she pressed her lips to the skin above the waistline of his jeans, she smiled at his muffled gasp. She wickedly flicked her tongue just inside the material, and he shifted, groaning softly. She smiled again.

His hands tightened in her hair, and he slid down the length of the bed to her, kissing her hungrily on the mouth briefly before leaving to nip at her neck and shoulders. Her hand went up to his arms, gripping firmly while his head moved down to her soft breasts. Tenderly kissing the top of each one, he moved between them to continue his path down her torso, slipping his tongue over her belly button and then repaying her favor by pressing his lips against the lace material covering her sex.

Her hips arched slightly at the surprising boldness of his kiss. She ached for more. He was pleased at how easily he read her body's request, yet he denied her. He moved back up to the soft mounds that he knew were awaiting his lips. He lightly swept his tongue over her, savoring the taste of her skin and enjoying her small gasps. Teasing her, avoiding taking her fully into his mouth, she was restless beneath him. He could feel her moist heat radiating against his jeans, and he longed to rid himself of the cumbersome clothing. His hands worked the rest of her body in a soft massage, his warm fingers against her smooth skin. The sensations she created for him were unreal, almost as if he were making love to a dream. Their bodies were in perfect sync with each other; it was more than either had anticipated.

Settling his mouth on her nipples, his warm tongue sent shockwaves through her. Her mind reeled from the

intensity of his touch; she felt her reality slipping. She felt an incessant need well up inside her, but not knowing what she needed or how to satisfy her desire, she became increasingly disquieted.

He immediately noticed her agitated movements; he felt her body pleading with him for more. He needed to taste her, to feel her deeper. She was already in his mind, devouring his body. His only thought was to extend the pleasure. He moved up to kiss her, his hand sliding down her belly and underneath her panties, through the soft patch of curls, to her moist lips. Without a sound, he slid his finger inside her, seemingly releasing her.

She moved against his hand, welcoming his entrance, finding only that she wanted more. She groaned against his mouth as he moved deeper inside, gliding in and out of her, stoking her fire and releasing her sweet honey. His thumb slid up to find her sensitive core, gently massaging. Her reality was now a distant memory. She couldn't think of anything except the swirling that had begun in her head and had now wound its way down her body to where his expert hand was pushing her closer and closer to climax.

The more she moaned and sighed against his mouth, the closer he came to ending her blissful torture. She could not hide her response. He wanted her like no other. He could barely grasp on the intensity of his feeling. Later on, he would compare this to an orchestra, all the right instruments coming into play at exactly the perfect moment, with only the sound of their music to measure their success.

Her hands had become restless again, roaming over his body, her kiss hungry and demanding. He applied a bit more pressure and elicited the wanted response.

Her breath was coming in rapid gasps. She slipped out of the kiss into a menagerie of feeling and sensation, her body aflame with pulsating nerves. She clutched tightly to his shoulders, holding onto him as if riding through a torrential storm. He could feel her convulsing against his nimble fingers and continued to work until her body lay still, her breathing quick. She felt him leave her, and her fingers tightened, but he slipped out her grasp. Over the pounding of her heart, she could faintly determine the rustling of clothing. She attempted to sit up, but before she could, his hands were on her thighs, pushing them apart. Still dazed from her previous climax, she did not respond immediately.

Having shed the remainder of his clothes, he could think of nothing more than tasting her. The need to have her on his tongue and between his lips overwhelmed everything else in his body. To be apart from her for the few seconds it took to undress was agony. Not wanting to break the tie the darkness had forged between them, he quickly positioned himself between her thighs and kissed the supple skin.

As his breath got closer, he felt her give way to a small quiver; she was now able to read him as he could read her.

She knew he was not finished and did not protest when she felt the tip of his tongue flick against her swollen flesh. She stilled herself, willing herself not to lose control so quickly. The only sensation was that of his tongue exploring the innermost depths of her body. It was enough to send her completely over the edge again, and as she felt his hands move to her body—caressing her, massaging her—she began to feel the delicious winding of that familiar coil. His lips and tongue were a neverending trespass to her womanhood. He licked and sucked and pushed his tongue inside her, demanding that she release herself to him once again. She was quick to oblige, her body nothing more than a tingling mass of nerve endings all in tune with his ministrations. Soon her body was responding in spasms of uncontrolled lust, her thighs quaking while his mouth lapped at the sweet liqueur that flowed from within. Sliding back up to her mouth, he kissed her deeply, feeling her heart race against his chest.

Still hungry for him, she gently pushed against his chest and moved herself on top of him. Not being able to see what she was doing, he felt everything and knew that at last his lust was about to be satisfied. Bending over to kiss him, she took his throbbing shaft in her hand and slid it up and down several times before placing it at her entrance. His hands on her waist, he spared no time and pressed himself into her. He didn't think anything could have been as exquisite as her coming on his tongue, but he was wrong.

Her tender slit was swollen from his kisses. She gripped him tightly, moving down his rigid member and taking in every pulsating inch. The feel of him—so complete inside her—sent her body into overdrive. She guided his hands over her breasts as she slid over him again and again. He felt her everywhere, inside his head, on his skin. He could not escape the rapturous vibrations she sent coursing through him. The ultimate delight in their blind fantasy was the heightened sense of touch, and it was being used to the point of being spent.

He could feel the muscles in her soft thighs as she flexed, twisting her body around him, milking him, sucking him, and caressing him. He thought he couldn't take anymore. When she slowed her movements, he realized he'd been holding his breath and let it out. Relaxing his body, he moved his hand up to her face and brought her down to kiss him. Still moving slightly inside her, she flexed her muscles, sending another new sensation through his lower half. He pulled her tight and rolled her beneath him, surging within her. He felt her deeper now; if she hadn't already penetrated his mind, she did then.

He lost sight of where her body ended and his began. Her fingers clawed at his back, pulling him harder against her, nothing between them but the feel of him inside her. The hunger electrified them both, sending them into an inexplicable tailspin. All conscious thought was suspended as they moved together, pushing and pulling. Their lips

found each other repeatedly between lustful cries and the sound of their bodies driving into one another. Thrusting into her, straining her flesh against him, he needed her; he needed to feel her pulsing around him in the most intimate release.

An excitement like never before unraveled within her, opening her mind and her body to his, taking his driving force again and again. She was overtaken by a sense of panic, a mindless freedom. Adrenaline rushed through her as she cried out his name, climaxing endlessly. Feeling his long, hard thrusts, she sensed his own loss of control.

Knowing it was upon him, not willing to let her go, he filled her, giving himself completely, pushing with a force beyond comprehension. The awesome satisfaction of being inside her overwhelmed him.

The intensity of what they had just shared hung in the air around them. The only sound was that of short, gasping breaths. They lay in each other's arms, the reality of what they'd done seeping into their exhausted brains. Sweat-soaked limbs clung to one another, not ready to contemplate anything else.

He reached up to touch the face he'd come to know so well within the last hours, not ready to relinquish his ghostly love to the light. She smiled into his hand, knowing she was thinking the same as he. Had she realized their rendezvous would be such the extraordinary experience, would she still have arranged the same terms? She didn't know. She didn't want to ask the same of him. She moved her mouth to his, wanting this last kiss, willing back tears. She did not anticipate such a sense of loss, almost as compelling as the experience itself.

He did not say anything but kissed her back, trying to convey his desire to stay, his arms wrapped around her, holding her to him. She pulled back. Turning away, she moved off the bed and closed the bathroom door.

He knew his request had been denied. He gathered his things and left, the door closing with a resounding click.

She heard the door close and left the bathroom, turning on the light as she did so. Readjusting to the light was difficult, but not as hard as returning to the bed she had just shared with him. His smell still clung the sheets, to her hair. She got up and returned to the bathroom, staring at her swollen red lips and tear-stained face. She asked herself, *Was it worth the experience?*

Cherry Pie

The lights were off, the light of the crescent moon casting a glow to offset the darkness. Her props were in place, and she was nearly dressed. The outfit she had chosen was sex kittenish without being trashy. She loved red and looked hot in it. She wondered why she didn't wear it more often. Sliding her stockings into place, she clipped them to the crimson garters and stood admiring her costume. The lacy corset was tight, but it accentuated her small waist and added a little something extra to her sumptuous breasts. She checked her hair as she stepped into a pair of matching stilettos. She had decided to wear her long hair up, mostly to keep out of her way while she worked, but it also gave a sexier quality to the ensemble. She gave a quick glance at her backside and smiled: taut and round like cherry tomatoes. Just then she heard the front door shut. Her game was about to begin.

She walked into the living room, standing confidently and waiting for him to notice her. There was only one corner light on, so it took him a moment to pick her out of the shadows. He began to walk toward her, and then he took a step back. Standing in front of him was not his sweet grade-school-teacher girlfriend. This girl, this woman, was a creature of the night. She was dressed head to toe in blood red leather and lace, with gloves, garters, stockings, and six-inch heels. The only thing he recognized was the soft, honey colored hair piled on top of her head.

He called out to her, and a slow smile spread across her lush mouth. She didn't answer with hello but stalked over to him and took him by the hand. Dumbfounded, he could do nothing but follow. She pulled him into the bedroom, the door closing with a soft click. His eyes attempted to adjust to the darkness while she pushed and pulled him onto their king-sized bed. He didn't realize what she was doing until his wrists were already secured above his head. She was working on his left ankle.

When he began to resist, her head snapped up, and she gave him a look that stilled him immediately. He didn't really know what her game was, but she made it clear that she was in charge. It excited him to no end. She finished securing his legs, leaving enough room for him to move about six inches in either direction. His hands, however, were held tightly together at the headboard.

She looked up at him and smiled. She could tell he was still in a bit of shock—after all, this was way out of character for her.

She held his gaze as she moved to straddle his waist. Immediately, he felt her warmth on him and glanced

down to confirm that she wasn't wearing panties. He was immediately astounded at the discovery that she was shaved. He felt a surge in his groin and saw her try to hide a smile. She knew what she was doing, and the fact that such simple movements were already making him squirm excited her.

She saw no sense in mindlessly undoing each button and instead ripped his shirt open in one swift motion. She heard him mouth an expletive under his breath and laughed. She ran her hands over his chest: hard, warm, with a smattering of dark hair. He worked out, and his body showed it. Her hands moved down to his pants and deftly worked them down to his calves. She loved the feel of his thick muscles under her hands and continued massaging his body, glancing up whenever he uttered an appreciation of her skills. When she had him good and relaxed, she moved off him and stood over him.

He was watching her intently, anxious to know what was next. He was not prepared for the show she was about to give. In a moment her hair came tumbling down in wild waves, and the beginning of Warrant's "Cherry Pie" filled the room. She began to dance, moving her body in an undulating rhythm to the rock music. She teased her leather corset open, taking the swollen mounds of creamy flesh between her scarlet-gloved fingers and taunting her nipples until they were ripe. He licked his lips, wanting them in his mouth. She continued the dance, finally ridding herself of the binding restraint. Turning around, she bent over to release her stockings, giving him a full view of a perfectly pink pussy begging to be fucked. If he wasn't hard before, he sure as hell was now. He started to pull at the tight restraints, needing to touch her. Left in only her arm-length gloves, stockings, and stilettos, she slowly wound herself down with the music. Brushing her hair to the side, she lowered her cherry red lips onto his hot, throbbing flesh.

At her first touch, he nearly came off the bed. Her mouth was so warm and soft, moving maliciously slow down the length of him. He could see her swallow every inch, and he moved to thrust into her sweet tunnel. She reached up and lightly raked sharp red fingernails down his chest in warning. She was driving him to madness as her wet lips and tongue slid up and around and down his cock. He wasn't used to taking the back seat in their sex life, although he wasn't going to complain tonight.

She slid her fingers between his legs, gently kneading the taut skin below his penis. His eyes rolled back at the new sensation. She watched him reveling in the unexpected pleasure. Her fire was building at his excitement. She could feel a growing wetness between her legs and hastened back to her task of driving him crazy. She knew he couldn't stand being restrained, but it stimulated her even more. She picked up the pace of her oral assault, taking him deep into her throat. She moved her other

hand so it slid up and down with her mouth, leaving no ground uncovered. He moved, desperately fighting the urge to fuck her naughty little mouth. She swallowed him several more times before she slowed, not wanting to end the delicious torture too soon. Painstakingly, she took her mouth from him and slid her body up the length of his, tearing a low growl from him with the feel of her satin smooth skin against his sweaty torso. Leaning close to his face, she brushed her lips across his, smiling at his futile effort to capture her with his tongue. She could see the veins in his arms as he was straining against her love ties.

She sat up, spreading her legs wide to straddle his waist once again. She leaned back, grabbing the tops of his thighs, and lowered herself on top of him.

As soon as she leaned back, he prepared himself for the inevitable. He felt the head of his cock pressing against the most luscious of openings. He could see her moist lips widening to accept him, and he frantically bucked underneath her. He needed to be inside; he wanted to bury himself.

But it was all her. She paced herself rhythmically, taking enough of him to fill her, but not as much as he wanted, she knew. After several moments of riding her hog-tied cowboy, she slid one hand between her slippery lips to feel him sliding in and out of her. She guided her fingers around the base of his cock and savored the sensation of her honey coating him.

When he felt her hands on him again, he pushed upward and caught her off guard, pushing a little deeper and hitting that spot inside her that made her eyes widen. She had been slowly building to her release, and the feel of his manhood pressing into her tender flesh sent white-hot lightening coursing through her body. She removed her fingers from him and began to ply her most sensitive area. Circling her clit with her middle finger, using light pressure, she felt the dizzying heat bubbling beneath her skin.

He watched in amazement, her tight body glistening with sex and driving down upon him with calculated motions, directing them toward a blissful finale. He was merely a toy to be used, played with, and he loved every minute. His own orgasm was fast approaching, and he could be still no longer.

Her breathing quickened as her pussy tightened around his straining cock; she was still in control, pumping him repeatedly. He pushed into her as much as he could from his confined position, meeting her writhing body. She began to unravel, tossing her head back and crying out his name.

He felt her quickening on top of him, and he had to have more. She barely heard the sound of fabric tearing over the sound of her own cries and their rapid breathing, but she definitely felt his strong hands when he grabbed her ass. He flipped her onto her back and drove into her,

filling her completely. He poured his seed into her as she came all over him, engulfing him in her sweet sex, his name torn from her throat.

Breathless, they both lay still, ripped scarves hanging lifelessly, one long glove tossed carelessly over a stiletto heel, and the room permeated with the scent of fiery passion.

'd been friends with these people for several years, and I couldn't count how many times we played truth or dare. It was something we did when the party died down and the craziness had stopped. Tonight was a night not unlike the others. We sat around Dana's living room, sipping our various drinks and talking about people we hadn't seen in a while, events that had occurred since the last party, and other idle drivel.

Johnny started the game. He turned to Dana, who was sitting next to me on the floor and said, "Truth or dare?"

Dana was typically the wildest of us three girls, but she started off with a safety: "Truth."

Johnny rolled his eyes, but fired his question at her. "Is it true that you've wanted to fuck Nate since college?" he asked.

We sat in stunned silence for a moment. Often we ventured into the sexual arena with our truths, but never on such a raw personal level. We all just took it as a respectful line not to cross. I snuck a glance at Nate and found him listening attentively with a smirk on his face. I shook my head.

Dana—not willing to break the rules—looked Johnny square in the face and said, "Yes."

Johnny tossed his head back and laughed. "Ladies and gentlemen, we have a game!"

Nate leaned back on the couch, a satisfied grin on his face, and I had a sneaking suspicion that he and Johnny were working together. Dana just smiled, but she had enough grace to at least blush. Sherry, the resident wallflower, visibly tensed, and I prayed the guys would take it easy on her. They weren't the ones I had to worry about.

Next it was Dana's turn. She turned to face Sherry and uttered those fateful words: "Truth or dare?"

Not wanting to get caught in the same situation as Dana, she opted for a dare.

Dana licked her lips and smiled. She glanced at Johnny and was met with a quizzical stare. She turned back to Sherry and very clearly stated: "I dare you to get Johnny hard only using your mouth."

I nearly came off the chaise. "Dana!"

I couldn't hide my shock that she would force timid Sherry into something like this.

Dana turned to me with a playful grin.

"Oh, come on, Anna," she said. "It's about time we livened this game up. After all, we are adults, aren't we?"

She flashed me a wicked smile, and I sat back down, still in a shocked state. Dana turned back to Sherry with an expectant look. I could see Sherry fidgeting in her seat; she was excited at the thought but afraid to accept the dare. She kept glancing at Johnny, whose bright blue eyes were fixed on her. Finally, she got up and walked over to him, kneeling between his legs. His eyes widened at her acceptance of the dare. She didn't look up at him but reached behind her and held her shoulder-length blonde hair back with one hand. Johnny quickly undid his pants and leaned back, giving Sherry the go ahead. She buried her head between his legs, tentatively licking at his already twitching penis. We all watched in shocked silence as our shy friend sucked Johnny to life.

It didn't take long before Dana came up behind her and gently took Sherry's head in her hands and pulled her out of Johnny's lap. Sherry smiled broadly with slightly swollen lips as she gazed upon Johnny's erection. He chuckled and quickly tucked himself in his pants. Sherry sat back down and glanced around the room, choosing the next victim in our sexual game. I watched her pass a mischievous look over our friend Chris. Chris was probably the hottest guy in our circle of friends. I had been crushing on him for years but was not willing to cross the line of friendship. I tensed, praying Sherry would not reveal this secret information during our game. But she did not pick Chris. Instead, she settled on Ryan, who looked happily anxious that it was his turn.

"Truth or dare, Ryan?"

With a smug grin painted on his face, he replied, "Dare."

I could tell he was hoping to get some of the action Johnny got. Sherry knew this and turned the tables.

"I dare you to masturbate right here."

The crestfallen look that crossed his face was almost comical, but Sherry wasn't through. Turning to Dana, she said, "And I dare you to catch it in your mouth."

No one said anything about the double dare being against the rules. We were all too into the game now. Dana shot Sherry a pseudo-evil look and knelt before the now grinning Ryan.

I leaned back on the chaise, feeling warmer than I had half an hour ago. I watched as Ryan unzipped his fly and pulled out his hard dick. I registered a slight surprise at his size. I would have never thought he was so well-endowed. Before I could catch myself, I briefly wondered what it would feel like. Blushing at the thought, I looked away and caught a wink from Chris.

The more I thought about it, the more my suspicions increased about their attitude toward the turn of events. I put it from my head and turned back to see Dana on her knees in front of Ryan. Her hands were behind her back. He had one hand resting on her shoulder, and the other was sliding up and down vigorously on his now throbbing member. I watched, mesmerized by the obvious skill of his

own techniques. I'd never watched a man pleasure himself. I felt the growing heat between my legs and blushed again.

I watched as Dana flicked her tongue across the swollen head, and a string of clear cum fell against her chin. Ryan was making incredible animal-like sounds as he continued the fast-paced stroking of his cock. Dana continued lapping up the juice that oozed from the tip.

Finally, after what seemed like an hour of continuous pumping, Ryan tossed his head back and grabbed Dana by the hair. Shoving his engorged flesh in her face, he erupted into her mouth. The white, creamy liquid coated her lips and tongue. She swallowed several times as he continued shooting hot streams at her. Dana, ever mindful of the rules, cleaned up every last drop of his generous load.

He released her head and sank back down in the chair as she got up and walked back to sit beside me on the chaise. We were all quiet for a moment. The line we had all set had been washed away by Ryan and Dana's uninhibited performance. The quiet didn't last long as Ryan, in a quiet voice, directed the question at Nate: "Truth or dare?"

Nate's eyes widened as if he didn't expect to be chosen. *Aha*, I thought, *your teammates turn on you.* I shook my head and laughed to myself. Nate recovered quickly and chose dare.

"I dare you to fuck Anna with your tongue."

Immediately, my mind went numb. I watched Dana's eyes flash, and Sherry sat back, relieved it wasn't her. I sat there with my mind reeling, only faintly aware of Ryan's second request.

"Chris, you can help him."

I glanced quickly at Chris, surprised to see him already up off the floor, apparently eager to get in the action. I was faintly disappointed at his typical male attitude. Nate took a little longer. He appeared confused, but I didn't have time to dwell on it. Chris had changed places with Dana and was now sitting beside me. I felt his hands tugging at my shirt, lifting it up. Nate had positioned himself in front of me. I felt like I was underwater, everything was moving in slow motion, and Chris and Nate's undressing of me immediately threw my idle protests to the side.

Before long, my pants were off, and Chris was kissing my neck and playing with my erect nipples through my lacy bra. I glanced down to see Nate parting my legs, sliding them up to rest on his shoulders. I was so distracted that I couldn't be bothered to blush over my exposed sex. Secretly, I longed to come. I knew it would not take me long to achieve my desire, but I was still startled at the gentle touch of Nate's fingers spreading the puffy lips of my pussy. As Nate guided his warm tongue over my wet lips, Chris slid his hands inside my bra and cupped my breasts in his large hands. Still kissing my neck, he took them out and began kneading and squeezing my heavy mounds. He began to pinch and pull at my sensitive nipples at the same moment Nate unveiled my hooded clit. His lips closed around the

throbbing nub, and I groaned loudly. He sucked and swirled around it, eliciting a sweet pulse deep inside my core.

Chris moved his lips from my neck to my now protruding nipples and suckled one and then the other, moving back and forth between them. I was lost in a sea of erotic sensation. Nate pushed his tongue inside my waiting opening, and I pushed my hips up higher to meet him. My movement caused Chris to slip and graze my tender nipple with his teeth. I cried out at the pleasurable pain and heard him moan in appreciation. He then took to taunting the rock-hard pebbles, nibbling them excitedly.

Nate's tongue was pushing farther into me, teasing me from the inside, and I began to gently thrust against his mouth. My moans became louder, and Chris moved his mouth from my breasts to my lips, absorbing my cries with his tongue. His fingers were rolling my nipples between them, pinching them harder. I was arching into Nate's mouth when I felt the tightening in my abdomen. I pushed harder against him, forcing his tongue deeper inside. Chris felt my impending orgasm and increased the pressure on my already painful nipples. I screamed inside his mouth as I came on Nate's welcoming tongue, my body gripped by a series of sensual spasms. Nate held my thighs apart, licking up the juice that flowed from within as I settled into a blissful numbness.

I lay still for a moment, the realization of what I'd just done with my friends beginning to dawn on me. I didn't have time to worry about it before I heard Nate say to Chris, "Now I dare you to finish her off and fuck her."

At these words I moved to get off the chaise, not willing to be a pawn in their sexual games any longer, but I was pinned by Chris already between my legs. His sweet mouth on mine, I soon forgot I even wanted to protest. I forgot five other people were watching us. Within seconds, he was pushing the swollen head of his cock past the smooth, wet lips of my waiting pussy. I wrapped my legs around him, pulling him into me. My body slid over his easily, taking in the pleasant fullness of him. His mouth never left mine as he eased in and out of me. Rising to meet his driving manhood, I took him deeper, wanting more of him with every thrust. Completely oblivious to my audience, I begged him for more. He obliged, ramming his cock deep and hard, punishing my greedy hole. After several minutes of pounding into my supple flesh, he slowed and pulled his throbbing member out.

He pulled at my weak limbs, forcing me to stand. He slipped underneath me and turned me around. Taking his fingers, he spread my swollen lips and impaled me upon him. His hands on my waist, he guided me up and down his shaft, coating it with my private honey. I reached down and toyed with my clit, desperate to come all over his demanding cock.

Seeing my obvious excitement, he pulled me down to him. Leaning over him, his dick still buried inside my

hot sex, we kissed. I was lost in the wanton display and did not register the words he uttered to a member of our attentive group. I felt Chris slide out of me, leaving my pussy longing to be filled again. I was not disappointed for long when I felt my tender opening being stretched again to accommodate a slightly thicker shaft. I turned my head quickly to see Ryan behind me, a lusty grin on his face. I looked down at Chris and noticed his approving smile. He reached up and kissed me again, slipping his tongue deep inside my mouth. Ryan was moving slowly, pushing all the way in, only to pull all the way out. Several times, he ran his bulging thickness over the tight rosebud of my ass. The sensation sent a course of dangerous excitement through me. I glanced at Chris again, his expression serious.

"I dare you to let him fuck your ass."

I paused for a moment, wondering if I'd heard him right. My question was soon answered as I felt the pressure against my ass. I panicked and fought to get off Chris, but he had me by the arms while Ryan held my waist. Realizing my position, I relaxed and allowed Chris to slide back into my dripping canal. The pleasure of Chris's rhythmic fucking eased the way for Ryan to slowly enter my virgin ass. I bit my lip against the pain, but I forced myself to relax. Ryan had me stretched to the hilt, buried inside my forbidden hole, as Chris was encased in my throbbing pussy. They began to move inside me, pushing one and then the other, taking me back and forth. The sensation was out of this world; my senses were on fire. The pleasure mixed with pain, sending thrills throughout my womb. Four hands were on my body, guiding me over their veined muscles. Out of the corner of my eye, I saw a figure move. Johnny was now standing over me, his swollen cock in his hand. He shoved it toward me.

"I dare you to suck me off."

I opened my mouth in acceptance. All three of my holes were filled with male flesh. There was no time to think, only feel, as one moved out, two others moved in, rotating, pushing, and pulling my body. I couldn't get enough. My tongue lapped at Johnny, my pussy was filled with Chris, and Ryan raped my ass. They had dared me into sexual submission. I was their slut, to be used and fucked until they came.

It was Ryan first, my tight little ass too much for him to handle. He pumped into my puckered hole hard and fast, encouraged by Chris and Johnny. I moaned against the rigid penis in my mouth as Ryan shot his hot cum deep inside my ass. Feeling it fill my unknown tunnel, my pussy started to quiver, contracting around Chris. Ryan's intense orgasm was a domino effect. His salty mess dripping down my ass into my pussy, I bounced harder on Chris, daring him to drench my insides with his own milky liquid. He tensed beneath me, slamming up into me; I felt my muscles clench his demanding shaft, squeezing every last drop from him. I was still coming when Johnny shoved

his dick in the back of my mouth and more of the hot, sticky wetness coated my throat. He thrust several times between my lips, and I came again and again. Every orifice filled with cum; my whole body was one giant orgasm.

After I swallowed Johnny's entire load, he released my head, and I slumped down over Chris. I felt his arms lift me up, and he laid me back down on the chaise. He brushed the hair from my face and smiled, then leaned down to whisper, "Truth or dare?"

Key West

The balmy breeze from the ocean drifted in, bringing the tangy smell of salt water with it. The gauzy curtains drifted aside to allow the moonlit rays to fall upon the spent lovers. The sun had set long ago. The island was now quiet.

Slowly she started to wake, her surroundings unfamiliar, and she began to panic, fighting to get out of bed. A pair of arms snaked around her, holding her close. She felt gentle whispers in her ear and soft lips on her neck. His body was warm, and she cuddled closer to him, his arms still around her, holding her tight. A smile formed on her lips as she settled back into a peaceful slumber. He watched for a few moments, making sure she was asleep again. He tenderly brushed a stray curl from her face and bent to kiss her before falling back to sleep himself.

When she woke again it was to the rhythmic sound of the shower. She rolled over onto his pillows and inhaled deeply, taking in the very masculine scent of him. She smiled to herself, remembering the exquisite evening they had spent together. Blushing, she recalled some of the more intimate moments.

After only a few moments of remembrance, she could feel the heat building within her. She ventured toward the bathroom and opened the door slowly. She was immediately engulfed in the hazy steam. She closed the door quietly and stood in the middle of the bathroom. Shedding her robe, she stepped closer to the shower, hoping to catch him unaware. She tentatively pulled back a corner of the curtain, and her breath caught. He was standing facing her, his head back, his eyes closed. His hands were pushing water across the wide expanse of his chest, droplets cascading over his shoulders, down to his muscular thighs. He turned around to face the water and she smiled, liking the view. Gingerly, she stepped into the shower and came up behind him, encircling his waist with her arms, her breasts pressed against his back.

He jumped slightly, his alarm lessened by the supple body clinging tightly to his. He turned his head and glanced down, she greeted him with a happy grin. He laughed softly and turned around. Now facing her, he wrapped his arms around her waist and lifted her, her legs automatically going around his torso. Her soft lips met his, playfully caressing his lips. She smiled against him, and he took the invitation, slipping his tongue inside her sweet mouth. She locked her fingers behind his neck and pulled him deeper into the kiss. He responded by sliding his hands underneath her and giving her ass a firm squeeze. She let out a muffled moan and released her hands; he

pulled his head up and looked at her. Her long, wavy hair was damp, and her soft, fair skin was covered in goose bumps despite the warm water on his skin.

He turned and positioned her under the steady stream of hot water. He held his hands braced against her back, and she leaned into the waterfall, letting it soak her body. He watched in undisguised desire as the water cascaded through her glistening hair and over her lush breasts. He stiffened as she moved her hands over her body, stopping to toy with her hardened nipples. She dared a quick peek at his response to her teasing and couldn't hide her pleased expression. He caught her playful glance and gave a low growl, burying his face in her neck, kissing her. He came up laughing with a mouthful of water. She stifled a giggle while he sputtered underneath the steady stream.

He began to lose his grip on her, and she slid a bit. He shifted and pinned her against the wall to keep from losing her completely. Her head rested on his shoulder as he got his breath back. He leaned his cheek against hers, and she turned, her lips finding his. He tightened his arms around her, crushing her breasts to his chest. She groaned against the kiss, squirming in his arms, excited by the friction of her nipples against his chest. One of his hands moved up to the back of her head, the other squeezing her bottom, which was still pinned against the wall. The water falling over both of them felt hotter than ever, and the heat inside her was one the verge of overflow. Her oral prowess, coupled with her endless movements, had the desired effect on his body. His only thought was satisfying his lust for her.

Her hands were resting on his shoulders; she tightened her grip as he readjusted their bodies. Gripping her ass with both hands, he pushed her harder against the wall. Her mouth moved off of his, onto his neck and shoulders, anticipating his entrance. He guided her over the head of his swollen shaft, rubbing between her lips; she nipped at him gently when he moved against her clit. The motion sent throbs of pleasure through her.

She tried to repeat his movement, but he held her so tightly that she had nowhere to go. Sliding his hands up to her waist, he guided himself inside her. Her warm, wet heat yielded to his insistent manhood. He tossed his head back and surged within her; she dug her nails into his shoulders as he filled her. Moving together, they danced again, claiming each other. He continued to hold her, sliding in and out of her tender flesh, her intimate warmth taking him with ease as if she were made for him.

Feeling the familiar tightening in her deepest parts, she voiced her pleasure, but the cries were absorbed by the sound of the water hitting their bodies. Her desire was not lost on him; he held her closer and pushed her further, wanting to extract the delicious response she was so close to. She felt his grip tighten, and the friction on her clit heightened her passion.

Feeling her so close around him and taking all he had, he slowly began to unravel, with every thrust increasing their pace, pushing her further and further to the edge. Her fingers flexing into the muscles of his shoulders, she continued to cry out against him, her voice becoming softer and breathy as she got closer to her release. The deep timbre of his voice resonated off the shower walls as he moaned her name. The song continued until she was nothing more than one excruciatingly delightful sensation. He felt her begin to contract. Pounding her against the water-soaked wall of their confined space, he poured into her. His wet, surging heat sent her into sweet oblivion. Her whole body was wracked with the pleasurable spasms of release.

She clung to him, kissing his neck softly. His head rested on the wall behind her, his legs still shaking from the force of his climax. Slowly, he slid her down the length of his body, holding her up on trembling legs of her own. He opened his eyes to look at her. Her pink cheeks were flushed with heat, her eyes still smoldering. She was beautiful. She smiled up at him, fingers playing with the back of his neck. They finished their shower with tender affection and got ready to enjoy the rest of their day together.

Most of the day was spent in playful abandon, shopping and lunching at a local pub. At lunch, they discussed going to the beach for the evening to watch the sunset before she left. It was their last night together. It had been a wonderful three days. She was sad it was almost over.

They arrived at the water as the sun dipped into the horizon. She danced toward the lapping waves, barefoot in the sand, and he lingered behind her to lay down a blanket. After putting their stuff down, he followed her to the shore, watching as the ocean breeze gently lifted her hair off her shoulders. He knew it wouldn't be easy to see her go, but he didn't realize just how hard it was going to be. He put his arms around her shoulders, and she turned up to look at him. He took her face in his hands and brought his lips to hers, a kiss as gentle as the sea nipping at their feet. She sighed against his mouth as he slipped his strong arms around her, a chill running down her back where he trailed his fingers.

Gently, she pushed down on his shoulders, urging him into the sand; she stretched her body languorously on top of his. Resting her head just beneath his chin, she traced her fingers along his neck to his shoulders and down his arms. He loved the feel of her touch so soft against his rougher skin. He reached down and lifted her face up to his and captured her lips once again, this time in hungry passion. Her fingers intertwined with his, pressing into the sand.

Sliding her body over his, she pressed her hips into him, igniting his fire. He let go with a low growl and squirmed underneath her full-body caresses. Slipping from his grasp,

she glanced around to find the last of the late-afternoon beachgoers gone. She slid further down his body. Before he could protest, she had his already hardening cock in her hands. Her outrageous behavior shocked him into momentarily speechlessness.

He watched as her sweet lips circled his swollen flesh. His head rolled back as he let her warm breath envelop him. Then he was inside her, gazing into her emerald eyes and watching as he disappeared inside her mouth again and again. She continued the oral assault on his throbbing member, letting the warm air rush over them and the scent of salt and sand seep into their skin. When he thought he could take no more of the wet stroking of her expert lips, she left him, tantalizing his skin with kisses all the way up the length of his stomach and chest, coming to rest on his lips. He took full advantage of her straddling position and easily guided his hands beneath her cotton skirt. Shoving her lace panties to the side, he quickly found the slick wetness and parted her lips. Running his fingers over her, he toyed with her clit, eliciting a delightful moan.

Not wanting to waste the waning moments of their evening together, she positioned herself above him, relishing his hardness as he pushed into her delicate opening. Taking the length of him inside her, she held his hands on her hips as they rode together, driving in and out. Her body was a swirl of sugared honey, swallowing him, stroking, and caressing him in the most intimate of gestures. With no one to hear and the stars their only audience, they cried out against each other, bringing one another to the edge and back again, not wanting the night to end. In one final peak, she came, her nectar seeping over his raw manhood as he joined her in the ultimate ecstasy.

Holding her close to him—her breath still coming in short gasps—he didn't want to let her go. While the crescent moon rose higher in the night sky, the lovers fell into peaceful accordance with their fate and left the sandy rendezvous, leaving only the imprint of bodies entwined to reveal their torrid secret.

Key West ...
Seven Months Later

E very once in a while, she'd catch the smell of salt on
the breeze, and it would bring back a memory of two
bodies intertwined on the sand. Though she was fond of
the memory, it seemed like ages ago. She never actually
thought she'd see him again, but somehow she had agreed
to meet him again, tonight. Although it was on her turf
this time, she was still very apprehensive. Even the deep
twang of his voice sent her legs to mush and her heart
racing. After all this time, he still had a hold over her. She
was frustrated with herself for being so easy. Slamming
the phone down, she gathered up her purse and headed
out of the house. She needed to clear her head.

About forty-five minutes into her drive out to the beach,
she began to calm down. What was so nerve-racking about
seeing him again? Her thoughts whirled around her head,
slowly replaying their time together so many months ago.
Her chest tightened as she felt the familiar stab of pain as
she recalled how they had parted. She couldn't go back
there; she didn't want to relive that anguish. She knew
she wouldn't resist him, though. Despite her anger and

the brick wall she'd built around her heart, she wanted him ... had to have him.

She pulled into the nearly empty lot and got out. Grabbing a blanket from the backseat, she tossed her purse inside. She was determined to enjoy the sunset without a cell phone. She locked the car and pocketed the keys. Making her way down to the shore, she stopped midway to remove her shoes. Feeling the sand between her toes gave her an unexpected surge of emotion. What on her earth made her think coming out here would clear her mind of him? She kept walking toward the water, finally laying the blanket down a few feet from where the sand was damp from the effervescent tide.

The sun was about halfway down. The sky was a bold pink, with blazing gold clouds. There couldn't be a more perfect reminder of their time on the beach. A familiar ache began to spread through her body, and she tried to shake it off. She dipped her toes in the water and smiled at the temperate feel of it. The breeze picked up and she shivered, wrapping her arms around her body. She was struck by a vision of his arms pulling her to him, holding her. She sighed, blinking back a tear. Silently she berated herself; she thought she'd cried her last tears over him months ago. She was even more annoyed at the realization that the hurt was not gone—it had been bubbling beneath the surface all this time. Well, tonight was it. Tonight she would get the closure she needed from him, and that would be the end.

It had been a long time, and he had kept his distance as long as he could. He knew he'd hurt her, but he didn't know how badly. He was afraid she wouldn't see him and even more afraid that she'd bail at the last minute. His ego couldn't stand up to much at the moment, and he knew she had every right to refuse him or worse.

He stood, watching her walk down the beach, drifting in and out of water in her bare feet. Even from this distance he could see the tension in her body. Every ounce of him wanted to go to her to hold her and massage away the hurt he had caused her. He waited. She needed space. He knew the way her mind worked, how she rationalized and analyzed every emotion she felt. She never spoke without thinking. Sometimes that irritated him; he felt like she was too rehearsed. He watched her bend down and fish something out of the water. Her hair fell over her shoulders, catching the last of the sun's rays. The sun transformed her mahogany tresses into an array of deep russets and fiery gold, giving her skin a bronzed glow. He knew that once the sun went down, she would return to the moonlit goddess he knew her to be, the one he wanted.

He began strolling toward her. She must have sensed his approach because she whirled around and froze. He didn't let her stillness deter him. As he came closer, the icy green glare he anticipated was fleeting. The emotional struggle played in her eyes, a wicked, stormy jade clashing with cold emerald and melting into soft sea foam. He didn't give her time to react, pulling her into his arms, unable to resist her pouty lips. The kiss was urgent and reckless, her lips and her body surrendering to him. He held her so tightly, inwardly kicking himself for even letting her go in the first place. She belonged here, with him, always.

They sank into the wet sand as her fingers clawed at his shirt, ripping it from his body. He wasted no time in tearing off her T-shirt and bra. Their lips separated for mere seconds to remove clothing, only to devour each other again. On their knees, clinging to each other tightly, he laid her back on the sand and pulled his face away from hers for a moment. His fingers caressed her cheeks. Wiping away a tear, he looked at her, puzzled. He stared into her eyes, searching her soul for answers. She acquiesced by wrapping her legs around him and raking her nails down his back. He brought his lips crushing back down on hers. Pressing her body into the sand with his weight, her sweet tongue invading his mouth, hot, wet, and insistent. He allowed her to explore. Guiding, tasting, and reveling in the sensation of having her beneath him again, his hands wandered over her body. Her skin matching the heat of his own, he brought his hands up her sides and stroked her breasts. His violent passion welled up inside him; he wanted to take her now. He wanted to possess her, to leave his imprint inside her.

She arched her back at the sensitive awakening of her nipples. His rough hands over her tender skin increased the incredibly erotic sensations coursing through her. He pinched and pulled at her nipples, remembering how she responded to him. She didn't disappoint. The heat grew intense between her legs as he bent to sip at her breasts, as if they were cups of wine. She gazed at him in senseless wonder, a voice screaming inside her head that her body ignored. What was she doing? This was too easy—she couldn't give in like this.

He sensed her retreat and increased his pace. He would not let her go; she couldn't be allowed to crawl behind her walls.

She felt his lips tighten around her throbbing nipples and let out a small gasp of delighted surprise. God, he felt so good. She could think of nothing else besides satisfying the slippery wetness within her. Her fingers began to fumble at the front of his pants. He lifted himself off her slightly to give her more room to maneuver, pleased at her insistence. She wanted him as much as he wanted her; despite the past, the need was still between them, the hunger that could not be satisfied.

She forced his pants down and released his swollen member. He shivered as she encased it in her soft hands, sliding her palm up and down the rigid shaft. If he didn't bury himself inside her soon, he was going to explode. Gritting his teeth as she toyed with the sensitive, smooth head, he shoved her cotton shorts and panties down over her hips. The smoothness of her skin was enough to make him come. He counted to ten.

She saw the raw look on his face and ceased her teasing. The look in his eyes revealed something she'd never seen before. Her first instinct was to be afraid, but his gaze excited her. His animalistic intensity was arousing. She lifted her head to meet his lips, and he shifted her body. Her legs instinctively parted around him as his manhood pushed inside her without resistance. She gasped in delirious pleasure as he surged within her. Buried to the hilt in her silky heat, he waited, relishing the feeling of her throbbing around him, her soft body moving in sync with his. She began to get restless, and he moved again, pulling out only to bury himself again. Again the laws of nature guided them, their bodies dancing to the age-old song of the tides slamming into one another, their cries echoing off the dwindling sunset.

Her body arching into his and her nails digging into his back, she cried out once more, releasing her anger and frustration, letting go of their past. She quivered around him, her body undulating with wave upon wave of orgasm. He watched her face as she succumbed to the ecstasy. His own control took a nosedive as he felt her contract around him. He thrust into her once, twice more, her name thrown into the melodic waters as he poured his seed into her, his grip on her tightening.

They lay in the sand, clothes strewn around them, sand and seashells drifting over them as the water came closer. He held her to him, her breath random and ragged, her warm body pressed tightly to his. He whispered to her.

She smiled softly in the glowing aftermath, knowing this is where she would stay.

The Club

The beat was heavy as bodies writhed all around him in the foggy room. It was nights like these that made him love his job as a bouncer. He stood like a lord over his kingdom, knowing that at a nod of his head any one of these girls would be his. He'd been working there only a short time when he first discovered the power he held in his small role. Comp their drinks, give them VIP attention, and he could do what he wished. After a while, the game had grown boring—until a couple of months ago.

He didn't know her name. She only came in once a month with some friends, but hers was a face he couldn't get out of his mind. The other bouncers said it was a case of forbidden fruit. So far, she had repeatedly snubbed him, and that just made him want her more. She wasn't just another pretty face in the crowd. Aside from the tight body and cute ass, she had these amazing eyes. He could never really determine what color they were; they seemed to change with the music. He privately nicknamed her Kaleidoscope Eyes.

He felt a sharp jab in his back and spun around to see one of the bartenders nodding toward the door. Her hair was down tonight, brushing just past her shoulders. She was wearing a short black satin skirt with thigh-high stiletto boots and a black off-the-shoulder sheer top. He'd never seen her look so seductive. He nearly creamed his shorts when she walked past him. She caught his eye for a brief moment and smiled.

Hmm, first time for everything, he thought. *Maybe tonight will be different.*

He watched her sidle onto the dance floor and decided to head upstairs for the view. He settled into his post at the top of a staircase that led to the third floor bar, VIP room, and private bathroom. He gazed down on the scene, seeking her out, watching her fluid movements sync up with the heart-thumping beat.

A drunk trying to buy his way into the VIP room soon distracted him, and he left to tend to the matter. When he returned, his eyes scanned the crowd below for a flash of her blue-black hair under the pulsating lights. He was so lost in his search that he didn't hear her come up behind him. He jumped when he felt a hand on his shoulder. He glanced down to see who dare disturb him, and he was greeted with a luscious smile on her cherry lips. His gaze softened and he slipped an arm around her shoulders. He was careful not to give away his racing heart and nervous smile.

"What can I help you with tonight, little lady?" he asked in his best cowboy imitation.

She laughed and replied, "Actually, I was in the VIP room and the bartender told me there was a bathroom around here somewhere."

Jimmy the VIP bartender was a good friend of his and knew about his obsession with this girl. There could be only one reason Jimmy sent her out here to use "his" bathroom. He wondered if she knew the reason as well. He smiled down at her and gave her shoulder a squeeze.

"Sure thing, it's on the other side of the staircase, immediately to your right."

She thanked him and sauntered off toward the stairs. If his heart was racing before, it was about to beat out of his chest now. He watched her go through the door and hesitated a moment before he left to join her.

As soon as she closed the door, she started shaking. If what they said about him was true, he wouldn't make her wait very long. She hadn't been drinking at all that night and wondered where this sudden boldness was coming from. She took a look around the room, noticing its plush appointments, all done in black and silver. She thought it was very retro 1980s. The marble counter was a cool gray, reflecting the soft lighting around the oval mirror above it. In the mirror, she saw a black chaise lounge behind her, next to it was a small silver end table with a halogen desk lamp and phone. She walked over and bent over the chaise, bringing her leg up to adjust the thigh-high stockings she wore under her boots.

She didn't hear him come in and was startled to feel his hands on her waist. With her heel still resting on the edge of the seat, she turned her head to look up at him. He raised one eyebrow as if to question her seductive stance and said, "I see you've discovered my secret."

She laughed lightly and turned back to her boots. He stood there briefly, eyes roving over her shapely leather-clad legs. She lowered her leg and backed up into him, her tight ass grazing against his already hard cock. His hands immediately went to her breasts, feeling her nipples tighten under the roughness of his hands. He squeezed her harder, kneading her with an animal-like intensity. He wanted her now.

He turned her around, and her eyes met his. She saw the raw hunger and felt it against her abdomen. He backed her up against the counter and sat her on top. His hands on her knees, he spread her legs and stood between them. With one hand behind her head and the other sliding up her leg, he kissed her, devouring her lips. He soon came to the apex of her thighs and discovered she wasn't wearing any panties. Without a sound, he parted her flesh and deftly slid a finger inside her. Her moist heat met his probing touch and signaled she was more than ready.

Lost in his carnal kiss, she was only partly aware as he released his swollen member. With her head pinned to

the mirror behind her, he tucked his arms beneath her knees he brought them up to spread her thighs further apart. Her wet pussy open fully to him, he pressed his hard cock to her. He felt little resistance as he pushed into the tight sheath. She cried out against his mouth as he moved deep inside her, expanding the tender flesh to fit him. He tore his mouth from hers and looked into her eyes.

"Damn you feel good, baby," he whispered. She moaned as he reached down to grab her ass, bringing her just a bit closer.

"Mmmm, that's it, honey, take it all."

He fucked her harder and faster, months of sexual tension igniting between them. Driving him into her again and again, her nails were embedded in his shoulders, and her face was buried in his neck. The pace was frantic; she'd never been fucked like this before. She could hear the music in the background, pulsing to match his impaling thrusts. His movements became rougher and harder.

Suddenly, he pushed away from her and pulled her off the counter. He turned her around and bent her over to spread her ass and shove inside her swollen pussy. She was too startled to make a noise, but instead she watched him behind her. His hand was wrapped in her hair, pulling her head up. Their eyes locked in the mirror as he reached around and started to toy with her clit. Already throbbing and swollen, he knew he didn't have to push her far to make her come, and man, did he want her to come.

He glanced down to watch his cock sliding in and out of her pink flesh. The sight of her glistening pussy being pounded by his swollen cock drove him crazy. She felt his experienced fingers working her clit and felt that sweet sensation growing inside her, willing her to let go. Her breath coming in shortened gasps, she started to cry out. He clamped a hand over her mouth while he plunged into her.

Feeling her contracting around him, he fucked her harder until she came all over him, screaming against his hand. He continued the hectic pace, pushing himself over the edge. He pulled out of her to drench her ass in white-hot cum. For a few moments, they watched each other in the mirror, the smoldering embers slowly dying out. Still trying to catch her breath, she turned and asked in nearly a whisper, "Was it worth waiting for?"

He pulled himself together, slapped her on the ass, and said, "Hell, yes."

The Window

lay in the dark, staring at the ceiling and unable to fall asleep. The fan above me was a hushed whir, blowing a cursory breeze over my sweaty body. I had tossed and turned in my bed for about an hour when I noticed a light come on across the alley. I watched curiously for a moment to see who came into the room.

He was tall. Fresh out of a shower, his damp hair appeared very dark and blended nicely with his deep tan. He had a swimmer's body—lean but very tone. Immediately, I was attracted to this mysterious neighbor. I stretched languorously and curled up on my side to watch this man as he went about his nightly actions.

I watched him towel dry his hair, the towel at his waist slipping a little to expose a lighter shade of skin around his hips. I smiled to myself, feeling a bit naughty about watching him. I had every intention of turning over and letting the man have his privacy, but I was entranced by the powerful display of masculinity. He sat down on the bed and stretched to yawn, his body flexing, showing his defined muscles.

I felt warmer now, kicking the sheet off the rest of my body. I lay there, propped up on my arm and my hand lightly grazing my thigh. I wondered for a moment if he was going to put on pajamas as he walked toward a large bureau. I watched him with his back to me, again admiring the strong movement of muscle beneath his skin as he looked for something. I began running my hand over my own flat tummy, feeling warmer than before despite the cooling night. I continued to rub my hand over my body as he moved away from the dresser and set a small object on the nightstand next to the bed. I strained to see what it was.

He sat down on the edge of the bed with his back to me again, and I saw the towel slump around his waist. I wished upon wishes that I could see all of him. I ran my hand over my plump bosom and was surprised to find two hard peaks pushing against the soft fabric of my tank top. I glanced down to confirm my suspicions. My nipples were erect, showing noticeably through the white material. As I looked over my own supple body, I caught movement from the room across the way and looked back up in time to see him stand.

The sight of his beautiful round ass sent an excited shock directly to the increasingly wet heat between my legs. I blushed deeply at my reaction, but I quickly realized no one was here. I continued massaging the hard little kernels, squeezing them between my fingers and eliciting little shockwaves. I moaned, rubbing my thighs together,

the friction intensifying my desire. I saw him reach for the small object on the nightstand. I could not tell what he was doing, but his body only moved slightly before he turned around.

My hand immediately slid inside my panties. I could hardly believe my eyes—he was magnificent. I felt like an animal circling its prey as I licked my lips and eyed the juicy piece of meat before me. I wanted to touch him, to wrap my fingers around his thick fuck piece. I wanted to deep throat every inch of him. My pussy began to ache as I imagined being taken by such a delicious cock. I watched in wonder as he began to touch himself. I now realized the small object was lubricant. He held himself in the palm of his hand, slowly sliding up and down the rigid shaft. He squeezed his fingers around the head and a drop of clear liquid glinted in the light.

As I watched him, my hand moved lower between my legs. I could feel the heat emanating from my pussy. I pressed my hand to it while I watched him slowly stroke himself, his bronze body moving fluidly as he slid his hand up and down, his eyes closed and a concentrated expression on his face. I couldn't resist any longer. I slipped my fingers inside, and the heat surrounded them. I gently pushed my lips apart and began toying with my clit. I knew it was wrong to give in to my lust for the man in the window, but the more I watched him fondle himself, the more I needed to pleasure myself.

I closed my eyes for a moment, imagining his sweet lips caressing my clit. Slipping and sliding through my moist pussy, I couldn't get enough. My body was so hot and sweaty, and my other hand was pinching and pulling at my nipples. The heat was increasing steadily, and I continued to watch him. His swollen member was pulsing in his hand, and I could almost smell his sex on the breeze coming in the window. I noticed his expression change, and his body shifted to accommodate his increased pace. I felt the charged excitement, and I couldn't help but match it.

With my eyes on him, I pushed a finger inside my tight cunt and immediately wanted more. I pushed another finger inside and began slowly sliding them in and out. I shifted my body so I was no longer lying on my arm but instead using it to toy with my nipples. I watched eagerly as precum drooled out of the tip of his cock. I imagined opening my mouth and letting it pool on my tongue. I moved my fingers faster inside my pussy, still wanting more. Attempting to imitate his size, I forced another finger inside, stretching the tight opening. While I fucked myself with my fingers, I moved my other hand to play with my clit. The sensation was so intense I started moaning against my pressed lips. Quickly, I glanced to see if he heard me, and I was reassured that he didn't. His hand was moving faster now, no longer stroking himself casually. His hips were thrusting into his well-oiled hand, and he was biting

his lip with his head thrown back. I strained to hear any sounds coming from him, but I was denied.

His body was such a wonderful specimen. His legs flexing with each thrust, I was lost in my own wet dream. Fucking my pussy harder, pushing my fingers all the way to the knuckle, I filled my slurping hole. I pinched and pulled at my clit, settling to a quick counterclockwise motion with the forefinger of my other hand. I felt the crescendo building, the tightening of my abdominal muscles as I raised my hips slightly to meet his thrusts. I felt wild, abandoned. I wanted to cry out. I longed for something deeper, for something thicker. My pussy begged for a cock.

I slid my three fingers out and brought them to my mouth to lick the sweet juice from each one. I reached to my nightstand. In the bottom drawer was something I never thought I'd use. My hand fumbled around inside the drawer for a minute before closing around the thick toy. I brought it up to stare at it. I'd never used it before, deeming its size ridiculously large. But now it was exactly what I needed. I licked the shimmering pink dildo and was surprised at the lifelike texture against my tongue. I glanced over at my partner in crime and saw that he had slowed his pace again. I was amazed he hadn't come yet.

Keeping my eyes trained on the engorged member sliding in and out of his hand, I guided my assistant to the soaked canal between my legs. I ran it up and down between my pussy lips, teasing myself and still a little wary of whether or not I would be able to take it all inside. I watched him reach down with his other hand and begin to gently squeeze the swollen sac underneath his cock. I positioned the bulbous head of pretend penis at my entrance. Still playing with my clit, I firmly pushed it inside, wincing slightly at the stretching of my tender opening. Once the head was buried inside, I couldn't wait to have it all. Inch by glorious inch, I took it inside, one hand never leaving my throbbing clit. The velvety cock was nine inches deep inside my expanded hole. I couldn't help but begin to glide it in and out, leaving nothing but the head inside before I pushed in all the way inside again. It was so thick, filling me completely and then some. I moaned against the pressure, but I didn't want to stop.

My friend in the window had begun moving faster, his slippery organ disappearing inside the cavern his hand provided. I watched him, mesmerized by his rapid stroking, and fucked myself harder, bucking my hips to meet my own thrusts. My entire body was throbbing, and I cried out, tossing my head from side to side. The sheet tangled in my long legs and seemed to hold me to the bed so I couldn't escape my own blissful torture. I continued riding the unyielding rubber flesh, my moans becoming louder, and then I heard him. It was faint, but it was definitely him. His soft groans drifted across the short distance, and it only intensified my impending orgasm.

My eyes were glued to him as his body tensed with his imminent release.

I arched at the first wave of convulsions that swept through me. Shoving the cock deeper and harder, I rode wave after wave of ecstasy. My tight pussy squeezed relentlessly, shooting my juices over the engorged member. I pounded it deep inside my tender flesh, watching as his body tensed one last time and his face contorted. Throwing his head back, he let go a deeply satisfied groan as white liquid shot forth into his restless hand. He thrust several times, spraying hot cum up over his stomach. I closed my eyes and imagined him shooting his load deep inside my womb. I cried out again as I contracted around the stiff muscle pushing inside me. I continued driving the insistent toy until the last tide ebbed.

After a few moments, my body settled down, the shattering orgasm diminishing to a pleasurable throb. I stretched and purred like a kitten as I withdrew the coated love stick. I rolled over and looked back at the scene across the way, and I was shocked to see him staring directly into my room. The lights were off, but the moonlight lit a good part of the room. Could he see me?

I lay still, staring back at him, afraid to blink. To be continued ...

Cat's Meow

He brought his cat in a couple weeks ago. Typically, I don't look twice at cat guys. They're usually gay or have serious attachments to their mothers. Justin caught my eye at first glance, and with fluorescent lighting that's pretty good. He was tall, wearing a tight fitting Army T-shirt. His jeans were loose but still hugged his ass nicely. His blond hair was still wet from his shower, and it was all I could do not to trace his strong jaw line with my fingertips.

I was in my usual scrubs, grateful that I had chosen the teal ones today because they matched my eyes. When we took his cat back to the exam room, he kept touching my arm and flashing his killer smile. I definitely wasn't repulsed by his forward nature, but I was a little apprehensive about Dr. Mitchell's take on Justin's flirting. I let him continue and finally Dr. Mitchell left the room.

Within seconds, the cat had been displaced, and I was on the exam table. Justin wasted no time in ridding me of my scrub pants and panties. Thank heavens I was wearing cute undies. The cool, medicinal air swept over my hot flesh as his large hands parted my thighs. I was terrified Dr. Mitchell would walk in to find Justin's tongue buried in my pussy, but the excitement only proved to heighten my pleasure. As Justin's lips and tongue swept over my swollen womanhood, I trembled, the deliciously sweet sensations rippling through my exposed body. His soft, relentless lips suckled my clit, bringing forth another wave of bliss. My head kept turning toward the door, knowing the knob would turn soon and end our lusty display. Justin's tongue pushed deep inside my wanting pussy. I covered my mouth with my hand to muffle my wanton cries.

We both heard the low gasp at the same time. My head snapped to the door, and Justin raised his head from between my legs, my pussy juices glistening on his mouth. Dr. Mitchell stood there with a shocked yet faintly amused expression. I moved to get up, but Dr. Mitchell placed his hand on my shoulder and gently pushed me back down.

The emotions running through me were a jumble of shock, excitement, confusion, and desire. Justin immediately took Dr. Mitchell's cue and resumed his oral ministrations, and all my emotions were soon replaced with overwhelming sexual hunger. Dr. Mitchell leaned over the table and shoved up my top, revealing my lacy white bra. He slid his hands inside, the coolness of his fingers immediately puckering my sensitive nipples. I arched into him as Justin began nibbling my clit. No longer worried that someone might hear my cries, I moaned loudly.

Feeling my orgasm racing through my nerves, I squirmed on the table. Justin was now fucking my contracting pussy with his tongue. I cried out again and again as I released my honeyed juices into Justin's hungry mouth.

Before my body could even begin to recover, I felt the insistent head of a cock pushing inside me. I opened my eyes to find Dr. Mitchell standing between my legs, his thick muscle slowly easing inside my still gushing pussy. I opened my mouth in mock protest and was greeted with another probing cock as Justin pushed past my lips. As Justin fucked my face, I could feel Dr. Mitchell's large member stretching my delicate flesh to fit him. I was being fucked at both ends, and I loved every minute of it.

I knew another nurse or even a patient could walk in at any moment, and I still couldn't get enough. My boss shoved his demanding cock deeper inside my drenched canal. I slurped my tongue over Justin's engorged head, and I knew it wouldn't be long before I was swallowing his salty load. He was thrusting with force now, hitting the back of my throat every time. Dr. Mitchell was half bent over the table, buried up to the hilt in my hungry pussy. He slid in and out of my body in rhythm to Justin's motions. I felt him tense and was surprised to feel him pull out first and squirt hot liquid over my belly. His body still bent over mine, he thrust against my smooth, wet skin, shooting jet after jet of the creamy stuff. Justin was next. He grabbed my head and shoved his dick against the back of my throat, then pumped several times before filling my sweet mouth with his hot cum. I swallowed deeply a couple times, ridding myself of the evidence of his explosive orgasm. I lay there, covered in Dr. Mitchell's stickiness and tasting Justin's appreciation of my oral appetite.

Slowly, they helped me off the exam table. Justin's cat purred quietly on a nearby chair. I stepped over to the little sink and was washing off the traces Dr. Mitchell's infidelity when the knob turned again. We watched in surprise as one the other vet assistants stepped into the room.

Dr. Mitchell turned to her, and in his most professional voice said, "We're finished with this patient, Donna. You may have the room now."

Dr. Mitchell left, and Justin gathered up his cat with a wink and followed him out. Donna looked at me with a bewildered expression on her face, and I just shrugged. Turning back to the sink, I laughed to myself at what just happened.

I'm seeing Justin again Thursday night, so I'll let you know how that goes. Dr. Mitchell has been on his best behavior, but every once in a while, I catch him sneaking a not-so-subtle glance at my breasts. I just smile.

Swallow This

It was a dive bar on the south side. It rarely attracted any big names, but every once in a while, the barely lucid patrons were treated as guinea pigs for new material from a well-known band. Usually they were guys who got their start playing late-night gigs on Sunday nights or used to drink there after band practice. Mostly it was a place for wannabes to talk smack about some hole-in-the-wall record producer who was going to make them into a big star. Sometimes you ran into a haggard groupie who told half-truths about the rock stars she slammed with back in the day.

I went in there once in a while to chat with my friend Justin, who bartended there. Usually it was just a pit stop on my way downtown to the happening clubs. I grabbed a Jack and Coke from my friend and sat listening to a watered down version of "Bodies" from a tired-looking boy on stage. I sipped my drink while I waited for my friend to take a break. I barely noticed when the band stopped and some roadies started testing equipment. Justin motioned to me that it would be a few more minutes, and

I left to go check my makeup in the mirror. I was meeting a girlfriend later who had promised to introduce me to her boyfriend's supercute brother. I had dressed more casual than usual, wearing a pair of tight black satin pants and a black T-shirt with a pair of red lips sequined across the chest. The red contrasted nicely with my long, dark hair, and I had painted my own lips cherry red to match my shirt. I adjusted my makeup, shook out my hair, and headed back to the table.

Justin was waiting for me, so I sat down in a chair across from him with my back to the stage. We chatted for a few minutes while another band warmed up on stage. Several times, I winced at the shrill sounds coming from the amps, but I was pretty used to the mediocre talent by now. Several more minutes passed, and Justin and I joked about bands we had seen here, and then a slow guitar began to ease in between the conversation and drunken laughter. I didn't pay much attention at first—until it slowly dawned on me that the voice I had imbedded so deeply in my mind that I could recognize it in the loudest of crowds was making its way to me.

I glanced quickly at Justin to see a slow smile spread across his face. Almost knocking over the table, I whipped around in my chair and saw him standing not even twenty feet away from me. His long, blond hair fell around his face, partially covering his baby blue eyes. He wore a pair of ripped jeans and a muscle shirt ... just as he had fifteen

years ago. As he sang a song I knew by heart, I could only watch, hardly believing there were only twenty other people in the room with him and me. His smooth, bluesy voice rang out over the listless patrons as they talked amongst themselves. I was lost in a reverie of steel guitars, drums, and that Yankee voice with the slight Southern twang.

I didn't notice when Justin returned to the bar, nor did I notice when most of the room emptied as patrons moved on to their final destinations of the night. I was lost in him, watching his smile, the way his body moved in rhythm to his music. From this dark corner in a nothing bar in the middle of nowhere, I found my own piece of heaven. My plans with my friend were no longer a forefront in my mind.

After about two hours, the spell was broken when the sultry voice I had loved since grade school quieted. Slowly, I turned back around in my chair, taking a sip of my watery drink. I realized that my body ached from sitting at such an odd angle for so long, and I laughed at how ridiculous I must have looked sitting there drooling over him for so long. I turned to say something to Justin and realized he was gone too. I laughed even harder, amazed at the complete loss of time I had just experienced. I grabbed my purse to leave and headed to the bar to say goodbye to Justin, but I ran smack into a sweaty body wearing a white muscle shirt. I knew who it was before I even looked up. I stood there, frozen and embarrassed at my clumsiness.

Then that voice said, "Your friend asked me to bring this to you."

I felt something cold touch my hand, and only by sheer will did I not drop the glass of ice water. I slowly raised my head, forcing myself to look at him, knowing that I was blushing fiercely. He smiled at me, and I almost lost my balance. I quickly sat back down. To my growing surprise, he asked to join me. Sitting there in dumbfounded silence, thoughts racing through my head and questions overwhelming me, I didn't even notice he was talking to me for the first few moments. He had such an easygoing smile; it was hard not to smile back. As soon as I did, I felt immediately more comfortable.

We talked until the bar closed, trading information about our lives, our loves, and our passions. In the beginning, I had so many questions about his career, but they seemed to fade as I became increasingly interested in the person sitting before me. Over the course of several hours, he had transformed from an untouchable superstar to an exciting, intelligent guy. We found that we had many shared interests—our passion for our work was the most common thread. It was 2:00 AM when Justin gave me the sign that it was time to say good-bye. I felt like a very special dream was coming to an end. When I walked out into the parking lot, I knew I would turn back into just another groupie.

I was very reluctant to say good-bye. Before I could utter those final words, he offered to walk me to my car.

Quickly concealing the bubble of shocked excitement that rose to the surface, I smiled and quietly nodded. Gathering my purse, I waved a quick good-bye to Justin, and we walked out the door.

There was chill in the air, but it was not unpleasant. The night was clear, and I could see the crescent moon and a few stars twinkling in the sky. We walked through the parking lot in silence, my heels and his boots making muffled noises in the loose gravel. Reaching my car, I clicked the remote and unlocked the doors. I glanced quickly around. Not seeing a bus, I wondered how he got here. Before I could satisfy my curiosity, his arms were around me, and the sweetest pair of lips were pressed against mine. Too shocked to protest and too astonished to kiss him back, I stood there, my hands pressing tightly to the car to keep me from slipping to the ground. As quickly as he kissed me, he pulled away. Eyes locked, we stood still for a moment. I could feel my heart racing as the gaze gained intensity. He brought his hands to my waist, holding me gently to him.

"Do you want to go for a ride?"

"A ride?" I almost tripped over those two words. To where? Even better question, on what?

"Yes, a ride. Come with me." He took my hand and tugged on it slightly, snapping me out of my stupidness. He was walking quickly, pulling me along in his obvious excitement. We came around the back of the building and were immediately greeted by a beautiful piece of machinery, shining in the weak light, sleek and powerful. He climbed on with ease, motioning for me to follow him. Doing my best to straddle the chrome horse in my tight pants, I adjusted myself in the seat, sliding up close to him with a tinge of fear running through my blood.

When we were settled, the beast came to life beneath me. I clutched at him tighter and felt his chest shake with laughter. Slowly, we moved out of the parking lot and onto the open road, heading away from the city. Once away from the traffic, he opened her up, letting the animal ride free down the darkened road. I felt a sense of freedom. The wind rippling through my hair, the strong body in front of me and the deep rumbling between my legs, I felt charged. I rested my head on his shoulder and released my death grip hold on him. I relaxed. Enjoying the cool night air rushing over my skin, I breathed in the mixed scent of him and the thickening trees around us. He was warm despite the chilled air surrounding them. I instinctively pressed my body closer to his, letting some of his warmth seep into me. He turned his head and brushed his cheek over the top of my head. I felt so natural, so at ease with him on top of this growling metal machine. When he slowed down and pulled off the road, I was almost disappointed, but I didn't dwell on this for long. He pulled me off the bike and into his arms. This time, kissing him didn't seem so foreign. My body had been so

relaxed and peaceful during our ride that this just seemed a natural conclusion to such an experience.

Only it wasn't a conclusion. Standing on the side of the road, underneath a silver moon and on the edge of the forest preserve, I was sucked into a kiss I had only imagined in my dreams. He was soft and gentle, demanding and insistent, all rolled into one magnificent pair of lips. My arms curled up around his neck, and my body eased into his, while his hands slid over my back and curved under my butt to pull me closer. It felt so good to be here, to feel his body heaving with quick breaths that matched mine.

The charge I felt earlier on the bike was more intense, pulling at me to release it. I felt like a very small flame, my tiny sparks surging and flickering until I was a raging fire. I could tell he was feeling the same pull because of the restlessness of his hands and the deepening of his kiss. After several very long minutes, we separated and stared at each other in the darkness. His blue eyes clashed against mine, stoking the fire growing between us.

He took my hand in his and led me deeper into the trees, eventually coming to a small patch of clean grass at the base of a very tall oak tree. He took off the shirt he had tied around his waist and laid it down, then knelt beside it. He pulled me down to him, taking my face in his hands and pushing my hair back. I couldn't stand not kissing him any longer, and I pressed my lips to his, letting my bubble gum tongue slip between his lips, teasing his tongue with mine. My hands were running over his arms, his shoulders, and his chest, feeling the flat, hard muscle. The reality of who I was kissing and what I was about to do screamed through my mind.

His hands were in my hair, tugging my head back to expose my neck. His lips drifted away from mine and down the soft column, coming to a halt at the fabric of my shirt. Without thinking, I lifted my arms above my head and let him remove the inhibiting clothing. Almost immediately, his lips were touching my skin, and his hands were gently sliding over the satiny material covering my breasts. As his mouth moved over my body to my soft mounds, I pressed his head closer to me to experience the wonderful sensation of his tongue teasing my cleavage. Quickly, he slipped the straps off my shoulders and released the clasp at my back, setting free my hardening, darkened nipples. I blushed, feeling suddenly exposed. He covered my body with his own, shielding me from the coolness of the forest and offering up a reassuring kiss.

My own hands were inching his shirt up his torso, wanting to feel his skin against me. He sensed my urgency and sat up, letting me take it off. I sat, quietly running my hands over his bare skin, mesmerized by the taut body before me. He smiled, taking my hands in his and bringing them to his lips, and then laying me back down on top of the shirt-covered grass. He brought my hands above my body, holding my wrists gently in one hand as his other made a path down my body to be followed by his kisses.

I lay writhing beneath his oral onslaught, the mixture of his hot, wet lips and the chilly air setting my senses on overdrive. His mouth moved over the tops of my breasts, sucking sweetly at my ruby nipples. I felt the fire rise up inside my womb as his mouth closed over the delicate nerve centers. His callused hands were now softly kneading the smooth mounds. My body moved beneath him, enticing him, silently begging for more.

The grass and the leaves gave way to the weight of our bodies, making soft rustling noises amid the sighs, moans, and kisses. My own desire to taste him overwhelmed my desire to be tasted, and I playfully rolled him over onto the grass. I watched him, glimpsing the mischievous glint in his blue eyes as I blazed my own trail of wet kisses over his body. Lapping my tongue over his smooth chest, I left no inch unexplored. I teased his nipples into hard little peaks, nipping at him gently with my teeth. My hands were intertwined with his at his sides, making it impossible for him to touch me as I moved my sweet lips over his stomach to the soft line of hair that led below the waist of his jeans.

With nothing but my teeth and lips, I undid the button and very slowly slid his zipper down, moving the denim away from the neatly groomed patch of light brown hair. I heard a sharp intake of breath as I pressed a kiss against the skin just inside his zipper. He raised his hips slightly as if to offer himself to me, and I obliged. I took my hands from his and slid his jeans off. His naked body rested on the bare grass.

With expectant eyes upon me, I did not hesitate to move my warm lips to the large, rigid member before me. At my caresses, it became harder in my mouth, the swollen head pushing between my lips and disappearing inside my mouth. He reached down to brush my hair out of the way of his view. Amid groans of pleasure, his intense blue eyes never left mine, always watching, anticipating the flicks of my tongue and the deep sucking of my mouth. My lips moved up and down his shaft, taking him in and swallowing him, only to pull him out again and rub the head against my mouth, tasting the salty, clear liquid that seeped from within. He moved again, pushing his manhood into my mouth with insistence. I took him deep, sucking every hard inch of him. A low hiss sounded as I worked him again and again, my pace increasing, bringing him to a crest and then slowing. My tongue moved over the throbbing veins, licking him like a dripping ice cream cone. I savored the taste of him, slurping the clear liquid continuously oozing from the swollen tip. I rubbed it over my own swollen lips before swallowing him again. Releasing him slowly from my mouth, he took my arms and slid my body up the length of his, his wet cock leaving a dark trail on my satin pants.

He pulled my lips to his mouth, shoving his tongue inside and tasting what I tasted. He groaned as I moved my

hips against the bulge between us. My own sex had grown increasingly wet while I labored over his thick member, and I longed for his touch on my delicate flesh. He did not deny me. His nimble fingers removed what was left of my clothing, finally freeing my hot skin into the brisk air. His tongue still fencing with my own, his hands dug into my hips and began pulling me up his body, sliding my swollen lips over his enlarged cock, spreading them wide over him and teasing the wet slit that lay hidden between them. He flicked his head over my throbbing clit, causing a small cry to escape my throat.

Continuing to guide my body to a sitting position on his stomach, I pulled my mouth away and looked at him, giving him the opportunity to lift my buttocks and set me over his mouth. In shocked surprise, I didn't have time to voice anything before his fingers spread my pussy lips wide over his mouth, and his tongue was inside me. Teasing me, taunting me, his tongue moved over my most secret parts, his lips kissing and caressing the juicy hole. My arms were braced against the tree in front of me as his hands pulled me hard against his mouth. His lips uncovered the hidden nerve center and his tongue stoked the flame, flicking it firmly and sucking it with his lips. I could feel the quickening in my stomach. My thighs quivered, and my arms shook. Moaning, crying out against his expert touch, I wanted more, but I couldn't stand it. I begged him and pleaded with him.

Sensing my rising excitement, he lifted me again and turned me around to face the opposite way. He bent me over, pushing my head toward his engorged manhood. I took it in my mouth without question, savoring the distraction he now offered. He groaned as my lips washed over him. Taking him deeper into my throat, I gently massaged his soft sac. I felt his mouth on my lips again, his tongue pushing deeper inside my honey drenched pussy. At his insistent probing, I sucked harder, moving faster over him. He met my mouth with small yet forceful thrusts, choking me with his protruding member.

His lips moved over my tender, swollen clit as he sucked deeper than before. Spreading my swollen lips, he pushed two fingers inside me. The pleasure was so extreme that I paused in my own oral pleasuring for a moment. Slowly, he tantalized my luscious tunnel, pushing in and out, mirroring the motions I performed on his cock. He began to push harder, kissing my clit and sucking it between his teeth.

My head bobbed up and down on his distended manhood, the head dark and swollen inside my mouth. The clear, stringy liquid was streaming now. His thrusts became more demanding, pushing his cock all the way down my throat. He sucked harder on my clit. I felt the flame rising, reaching down into the deepest parts of me and setting my whole body on fire. My pussy began contracting around his fingers, and I moved faster. My lips

were a constant force around him, moving up and down, pumping him. He fucked me harder with his fingers and sucked harder on my pussy. I ground into his face, coming in his mouth as he lapped up the juices flowing from between his fingers.

The hard cock shooting off into my own mouth muffled my cries. I continued to milk him, swallowing all that he had to give. His moans echoed off the walls of the forest. His forceful thrusts slowly gentled into a slight rocking motion, until he stilled and I knew to move my mouth from his sensitive member. His tongue still licking, he softly caressed the round globes of my ass. I turned around to move off him and onto the soft shirt. He rolled onto his side, taking my nipple into his mouth and teasing it with his tongue. I moaned and turned into him, our naked bodies cradled against each other. We lay there, letting the sounds of nature surround us.

Slowly, we gathered our things and dressed. I shook the leaves from my hair, and he did the same. We grinned at each other. He took my hand and led me back to the bike. Before I climbed on, he pulled me to him and kissed me hard on the mouth until my panties began to grow wet again. We got back on the bike and took off back toward the bar and my car. Holding on to him now seemed even more natural than before. I closed my eyes and let the wind engulf me again; breathing in deeply, the smell of our sex and the fresh grass clung to the fabric of his shirt.

We sped down the road, leaving the secrets of the forest behind and arriving back at the empty parking lot.

He parked next to my car and climbed off, lending me a hand. I walked to the car door and tossed my purse inside and turned to say good-bye. Instead, I was met with another soft kiss, his arms wrapped around me, pinning me to the side of the car. His lips and tongue moving over and inside my mouth felt like a part of me. His kiss became insistent as he pushed my T-shirt up to fondle my breasts and then pushed my pants off my hips. His hand eased between my thighs. Pushing my still swollen lips apart, his fingers found my core and teased it to fullness. I groaned against his mouth and reached for his own swell of manhood. I slid my hand down the front of his pants and found his large member ready and willing to greet my masterful hands. I stroked him steadily as he teased and pinched my clit, forcing the ache in my pussy to grow.

With a sense of urgency, he lifted me up without breaking contact with my wet flesh below or my hot lips above. He walked around to the front of my car and set me down. Turning around to face the windshield, I bent over the hood while he shoved my pants down and spread my legs as far as they could with the bindings at my ankles. I heard the zipper of his jeans and immediately felt his swollen cock probing the entrance to my tight hole. I wanted all of him now; I wanted him to fuck me hard and fast.

He pushed inside, stretching my tender opening. I voiced my pleasure at the throbbing thickness inside me. He moved agonizingly slow at first. I pushed back on his cock, trying to take more of him faster, but his hands were hard at my hips, keeping his own pace. He kept his steady, slow pace for a few more minutes, seeming to taunt me. Moaning and sighing at the exquisite pleasure, I pleaded for more. Finally, his fingers digging into my flesh, he increased his thrusts, pushing deeper inside me. My breath caught as he filled me repeatedly, shoving me over that perilous edge. His groans incited my sexual pleasure, and I begged him for more, wanting it even harder. He did not disappoint, slamming his cock into my dripping hole. He was now bent over me, his hands on mine on top of the hood of the car. Fucking me in the middle of the brightly lit, abandoned parking lot, I was excited beyond my wildest dreams. He continued to push in and out of me, bringing me closer and closer to that all-engulfing fire. I felt him become frantic in his pace; the sound of our bodies slapping together was the only noise in the night. He stiffened and pulled his swollen head out of my gaping hole. Quickly, I was turned around and pushed to my knees. The bulging head of his cock pushed past my lips. After a few sharp thrusts, my tongue was covered in the creamy white liquid. I lapped it off the swollen head and licked my lips, swallowing him for a second time tonight.

I smiled up at him and caught his grin as he lifted me up and onto the car. Soon he was down in front of me, my legs spread and my pussy bare to the night. Before I could really feel the chill, he covered it with his mouth, bringing back the throbbing I had felt only moments before. He had barely pushed three fingers inside me before I felt the familiar quickening. I pushed my hips higher, forcing the pressure of his tongue on my clit and his fingers deeper inside as I came again in his mouth. My honeyed juices flowed onto his tongue, and he drank from me until another wave of pleasure overwhelmed my body, and I had to bite my tongue from crying out. My head tossing from side to side, he brought me to another peak, higher than the first two as his fingers pushed deeper inside me. My whole body tightened and released, finally resting in a blissful state of ecstasy on top of the car.

He stood up and sat next to me, his hand on my leg. He leaned over and laid a soft kiss on my lips, placing the shirt he had tied around his waist on my shoulders. I watched him get on his bike. He gave me a playful salute and rode off. I slipped my arms inside the sleeves and caught a whiff of grass, sex, and rock and roll. I smiled to myself and slid off the car.

The Kiss

The invasion started slowly, soft and unassuming in its intent. My body was tense against his, strong confident hands as they massaged my skin, urging me to relax. I was afraid, fearful of the intensity that threatened to devour me. Gently he parted my lips, not pushing between them just yet, but stroking them, wetting them with his tongue, and readying my hot flesh for his entrance. My senses were awash with the subtle sensations streaming through me. I relaxed at the insistent coaxing of his mouth. It was impossible to be still. My hands gripped him, pulling him closer to me, silently begging for more. My entire body hungered for him. He was taunting me now, kissing outside my lips, nipping at them.

His nibbles subsiding, he shifted his body slightly. I felt the tip probing at the opening of my sweet lips. Softly, he parted them, sliding between them with ease. At first taste, I sighed, the gentle sweetness of his slow entrance tugging at my heart. I dug my fingers into him, trying desperately to pull him deeper into me. He was sure in his pace and resisted my quiet plea. He was slow and constant, milking every twist and turn of my body for the seductive response it was.

My breasts pressed against his hard chest, my stiff nipples grazing across him as we moved together. I was lost, slipping and sliding in rhythm to his driving invasion. I anticipated every agonizing caress, always thirsty for more. He could not satisfy my craving for him. I opened wider, accepting all that he had to give. The teasing had long ago ceased, his hunger for me morphing into a carnal possession.

Everything disappeared, two souls intertwined on the edge of a sensual oblivion. I could be falling, but there was no fear. He held onto me, as lost in this moment as I was. We crossed over each other, mingling our heightened senses. It became so that I no longer knew where he ended and I began, and when I thought I could take no more of the tortured bliss, he released me.

Overwhelming sadness engulfed me as I registered the emptiness of my body without his. I reached out for him, his hands caressing my face. I opened my eyes. Staring directly into his eyes, I watched the remnants of our kiss fade away. Tears welled up inside me, only to be chased away once again by the soothing caress of his lips on mine.

Sexcraft

She sat cross-legged on the ground with the large book in her lap, her palms up on either side. Her head tilted up toward the cloudy night. He watched in stunned silence as her chest rose and fell and the clouds parted to reveal the light of the blood moon. As is typical of harvest time, it was large and round, tinted with the rusty color of the fallen leaves. She rose, letting the book fall to the grass and keeping her palms up as she moved her arms up toward the glowing sphere. He watched intently as her lips moved, breathing the seductive whispers of the ancient art. Chills raced up his spine as a breeze whistled through the clearing. Seeing her blonde hair flutter around her shoulders to reveal pale, smooth skin, his groin stirred. He turned to leave, feeling guilty for disturbing her midnight ritual. The leaves crackled beneath his feet. He cringed.

In a swirl of gossamer and gold, she was upon him, her aquamarine eyes on fire. She didn't speak, but it was clear she was not happy about being interrupted. They stood for a moment, staring at each other, then she bent her head and pressed her lips to his. The unexpected gesture took him by surprise, but it was the feel of her lips that nearly knocked him to his feet. She was warm and soft, almost like she was melting into him. The feeling was incredible. He placed his hands around her slender waist and pulled her closer to him, again feeling that she was merging into him.

So deep into the kiss he fell that he did not realize she had led him to the circle where he had first spotted her. She stepped away from him, her eyes never leaving his. She lifted her arms again and whispered words into the wind that seemed to dance around them, fluttering the leaves and the trees. The air was charged where it had been cold only moments ago. He had been concerned about her thin garments; now he could only wonder if she was as hot as he was. She stepped closer to him, placing her hands on his chest. He looked down at her hands and shook his head. For a moment, he thought he could see through them. Bringing his eyes back to hers, he was instantly reassured by the inviting twinkle in her sea-green depths. Covering her hands with his, he helped her ease his jacket off his shoulders. Her fingers lingered on his subtly defined biceps as the jacket slipped off onto the grass. He smiled, pleased that she liked what she touched.

He slid his own hands underneath the heavy corn silk tresses and brought her lips back to his. Everything he touched of her felt like melted chocolate, like sinking

his fingers into warm marshmallow. He couldn't stop touching her; his hand caressed her heart shaped face, running over her shoulders and all the way down to the tips of her long, blood red nails. Every inch of her body against him fit perfectly. They sank to their knees, and she pushed against his shoulders, a small smile on her lips. He sat back on his heels and waited for her. She stood up again and raised her arms once more; this time he could clearly hear the melodic sounds of an ancient language roll off her tongue. He was mesmerized by this midnight angel. He watched as she spoke into the night, and warmth crept through his loins. So entranced by her charms, he did not notice at first the second and third pair of hands beginning to strip him of his clothes. The feather light touches were fleeting but welcomed.

Awareness of their presence first arose as a pair of luscious lips pressed warmly to his neck and another caressed his naked chest. He looked down and was greeted by a set of thick, dark eyelashes surrounding liquid pools of amber. Her hair, like molasses, spread enticingly over the rest of his nakedness. Unaware of where this girl came from, he looked to his blonde goddess for answers and was instead met with almond shaped eyes the color of midnight. A laugh like bubbling champagne echoed over the clearing as his mistress came back into view.

She stood in front of him, the moonlight behind her showing the distinct outline of her body through her thin lavender gown. Immediately, he felt himself stiffen at the vision she presented. A flush crept onto his cheeks at the full realization of his position.

All three girls now stood before him like goddesses from some far-off land. His long-lashed friend with the delicious caramel colored skin knelt in front of him, sliding herself between his legs and up his body to slip her tongue inside his mouth. Accepting her kiss wasn't a conscious decision, but how could he resist? Her lush breasts heaved against him, and his hard shaft pressed tightly against the junction of her thighs, straining against the sheer fabric that acted as a barrier. After what seemed like an endless ride on her cinnamon kiss, he felt her pull away.

Before disappointment could set in, her body slid down his and the plump bubble gum mouth of the mistress with the midnight eyes and fiery red hair settled into the crook of his neck and began to suckle gently. The sweet smells of their combined perfumes were intoxicating; he felt drunk but not hazy, and the visions of these lovely ladies were clear as crystal. His eyes sought out the golden haired one, and he was met with an approving smile as she gazed down at him and the two concubines who were slowly, meticulously covering every inch of his body with their smoldering kisses. She stepped around the scene and knelt at his head, smoothing his hair off his face. She whispered more words in the entrancing tongue he didn't recognize. She bent lower to whisper to him and

nuzzled her supple breasts against his cheek. He moaned at the excruciating, erotic touch and relaxed into a sleepy delirium as the three ladies moved around him, touching, kissing, caressing.

The carousel of women continued for some time, each taking turns tasting his skin. The relaxed state slipped away as the kisses became more urgent and the heat of their bodies increased. As if on command, a breeze drifted into the circle, blowing away the thin sheers covering the girls as if they were made of nothing but clouds. His eyes widened in appreciation as he gazed at the beautiful array of skin before him. His blonde mistress with her moonlit glow and matching hair; his molasses candy still working on his lower half and proudly displaying large breasts with dark rosy nipples; and of course the siren with long legs the color of warm honey. A sense of urgency pulsed through him as the trio shifted positions. It was now the spicy redhead who knelt between his thighs while the other two lay on either side of him, taking turns kissing his mouth, his neck, and his upper body. He moved his hand over the smooth backsides of either girl beside him and moaned in appreciation of their skillful mouths.

After a moment of watching sugar and spice tease and taste, the third mistress dipped her head close to his swollen shaft. He could feel her breath on him and stilled in agonizing anticipation. Slowly, she slid her tongue around the sensitive head, his breath quickening as he watched. She gazed into his eyes as she pressed it to her lips and took him inside her mouth. He let out a quiet hissing sound as a billion nerves went off in his body like firecrackers.

Staring intently at her while she sucked and swallowed his protruding flesh, he failed to notice that the other two had stopped their oral delights and were partaking of each other's tender kiss. His gaze shifted to the two beauties above him, wrapped in each other's arms in a gentle exchange of lips. His pulse quickened as their kiss deepened. The pale tresses clashed with chocolate curls as their tongues met in fevered passion. He watched in amazed silence as they sought out each other's touch, ivory hands on dark skin, bronzed fingers tweaking pink nipples.

His focus shifted as the body between his legs took him out of her mouth and sat up. He could see her eyes on fire as she watched the exchange above her. Quickly, she slid up the length of his body to capture the full lips of the golden mistress. Without uttering a sound, the dark goddess moved behind her, pushing the fiery locks to the side and leaving a trail of wet kisses down her body. Despite the absence of direct contact with his own body, he felt strangely mingled with the tantalizing display of feminine sexuality. The languid movements of the women continued as they draped each other with tender touches and wet kisses. Dark skin blended with light, crimson hair

intertwined with coffee, each contributing her own scent to the seductive aroma of sex. He inhaled deeply, taking the intoxicating fragrance of the girls inside him.

Watching their hands and bodies slide over each other seeming to overlap their movements were so rhythmic, so in tune to everything around them. His senses were on fire as their supple skin brushed him, teasing him as they stroked each other. Slowly, they began to include him in their pagan love fest, trading kisses with the others then sharing in the warmth of his mouth. Soon, he felt the feather light kiss of his fair maiden on his engorged member and reached out to touch her hair. His fingers slipped through it as though it were made of air. Before the puzzle could sink in, the other two were partaking of his mouth again, slipping their saucy tongues inside his mouth, parrying with each other, licking his lips and taunting him. The exquisite torture seemed to go on forever. His body was becoming increasingly tense with every kiss, every touch and stroke. His natural instinct to bury himself in one of these fine angels moved quickly through his head, and he began to get restless.

She must have sensed his discomfort, because the pagan princess with her lips wrapped so delicately around his shaft moved her body over his, and he was suddenly engulfed in the sweetest sensation. She fit him perfectly, like soft, warm silk. He watched as she tossed her head back, her hair cascading down her back and her breasts jutting proudly under the glow of the moon. Both mistresses turned their attention toward her, taking her pointed nipples into their mouths and suckling as she rode him. His eyes widened in ecstasy as the women worked their magic on him. As good as the sensation of the blonde wrapped around his throbbing manhood was, watching mistresses crimson and caramel was beyond his imagination.

As each of the ladies nipped and sucked at each other's breasts, they all took turns offering their most intimate caresses to his heated member. The sweet, silky embrace was the same, only the faces changed. He watched in amazement as the scarlet haired Amazon reached for the pale tuft of hair between the blonde's legs. Gently, she parted the slippery, swollen lips and slid a finger inside. Probing for a moment, she withdrew her hand and tasted the glistening drops that clung to her fingertip. A slow smile spread across the face of the coffee colored queen, who was currently displaying her technique on his ever-willing shaft. She also dipped a finger inside the fair one to taste of her essence.

His mind was whirling with thoughts and sensations as the girls shifted positions again. He was now lying between the supple thighs of his golden goddess, his probing staff nestled at the tender opening of her womanhood. Unable to resist temptation, he slid inside her. She opened completely to him, allowing him to bury himself deep

inside her womb. As he surged in and out of her lithe body, the dark tendrils of his bronze maiden brushed against his face while she explored his mouth once again. Hearing a muffled sound from beneath him, he glanced down to see her sweet mouth buried between the nether lips of the goddess before him. He watched as she pushed her tongue inside the girl. Turned on beyond belief, he drove harder into the wanton angel.

Turning his head, he found the siren kneeling next to him, her legs spread while the fingers of both women plied the wet lips, eliciting subtle moans from her juicy mouth as it nibbled on his neck. Barely catching his notice, the breeze had picked up into a substantial wind, the leaves no longer a light fluttering but racing around the clearing. The trees bent to the whim of its call, and the moon appeared to glow brighter, shining a spotlight down on the lustful foursome. Nails bit into his back as mistress mahogany's cries reached a fevered pitch in answer to the golden goddess's expert tongue. As her cries reached higher, it was the maiden of fire whose melodic tones coupled hers, together carrying on the wind the sounds of a powerful sexual energy. Encouraged by their throes of passion, he drove deeper into the hot chasm of the woman beneath him. Feeling her body contract around him, the air immediately charged and seemed to explode as her joyous calls joined her sisters. His body rife with unintelligible bliss, he released the long awaited orgasm, pouring his seed into the fair maiden who first stirred his passion.

He collapsed onto the girls, his body spent and his mind reeling. He lay motionless; only the sound of his ragged breathing echoed through the clearing. He lifted his head, seeking out the alluring eyes of one of the witches who so captured him. He found only the shadows of the trees beyond. Quickly, he sat up, glancing around him and searching for any sign of the ladies. Neither a chocolate curl nor a gossamer slip of lavender to be seen, he shook his head in disbelief. Gathering his clothes, he briefly wondered if could have dreamt such a delicious trio. Keeping his eyes peeled, he finished dressing. As he shrugged his shirt over his shoulders, he winced in pain, feeling the faint red welts left behind by nails gripping him in the throes of passion. Walking back toward where he had first spotted the pale blonde, he turned around, tossing a questioning glance back at the circle where he'd lain with three seductresses only moments ago. Shaking his head once again, he walked off, the echo of sultry giggles carried on the breeze.

Wild Ride

There were only about seven people on the bus in addition to themselves. Being later in the evening, that was pretty normal. They had just come from dinner downtown and were heading back to her place for the night. She was looking forward to warming up, but as they boarded, it appeared the heater wasn't working because it seemed as cold on the bus as outside of it. She hadn't really dressed for the weather but for him, wearing only her leather jacket over a thin silk top and black pleated skirt. Her legs might as well have been bare for all the protection her stockings offered. They didn't get to see each other as often as she would have liked. It was nearly a seven-hour drive to the Keys from Orlando, so she made a special effort when they were together. She knew he appreciated it.

The bus was mostly dark. Two gentlemen sat kitty corner across the aisle from them, and she could see a young couple a few rows ahead of them laughing. Although there were plenty of empty seats available, he pulled her into his lap as they sat down. He knew she was cold—she usually was—and they made a perfect pair because he was always warm. She turned to face him and slid her hands inside his coat, her icy fingers warming immediately. He put his arms around her, pulling her closer, trying to stave off some of the frosty air that surrounded them. She rested her head on his shoulder, relaxing into his strong body.

Their faces were so close she could smell the hint of the after-dinner mint on his breath. He smiled down at her, losing himself in the liquid green of her eyes and softly brushing the loose tendrils off her face. His warm touches sent more shivers down her spine, but they were pleasantly welcomed. She lifted her lips up to his, lightly brushing against them. Before she could move away, he brought his hand up to her hair and held her. There was a flash of jade as her eyes widened and he deepened the kiss. Her hands moved up to encircle his neck, giving herself to the tender dance. Both his arms went around her, pressing her tightly to his body.

A gentle warmth started to spread through her, slowly melting away what was left of the winter chill. She trailed her tongue along his succulent lips, inviting him to taste her. He didn't hesitate to respond, slipping his own tongue into her mouth. She moaned softly against his mouth, tracing her fingers along his neck and back down to his chest, where she could feel his heart beating quickly through his shirt. She undid the top few buttons, sliding her fingers inside. Her cool hands on his hot skin sent a jolt through him. He was so lost in her kiss that he didn't feel her undressing him.

He slowly withdrew from her mouth; she glanced up, getting lost in the amber depths that pierced her soul. She became aware of his fingers discreetly inching their way up her blouse. She placed her hand over his, and when he started to protest, she placed one finger on his lips. Without breaking their gaze, she shifted one leg over to the other side of his so she now sat facing him with her thighs on either side of his. A slow smile spread over his face as she removed her hands from his and placed them on his shoulders. They were now eye level, and the glint of mischief in her eyes only sparked his imagination. Did they dare?

He didn't think she would go that far, especially with other passengers sitting no more than four feet away, but she didn't show any signs of stopping as he continued his journey to find the soft, satiny fabric of her bra. He slipped his hands underneath it, and she gave an almost inaudible gasp. Her body trembled beneath his expert touch, the soft flesh of her breasts tightening as he delicately plied her. Increasingly mindful of her wanton display, she leaned into him, pressing her swollen lips to his to cover her body's reckless response to his ministrations.

He smiled inwardly at her sudden shyness and proceeded to rub his rough palms over her berry-like nipples. He longed to pull them into his mouth and suckle the sweet pebbles, but he settled for the frustrated groan she expelled when he rolled them between his thumb and forefinger. She could feel dampness beginning to spread under her skirt, and she could feel his hardness tightly pressed against the inside of her thigh. In rhythm with their kiss, she began to subtlety move in his lap. The sudden friction gave him a start, and he took his mouth from hers.

So this is how she wants to play, he thought.

Leaving her breasts tingling with sensation, he brought one hand up and wound it around her long satin curls; the other hand he moved to her hips, under her skirt to touch the top of her stocking. Toying with her bare thigh for a moment, he moved on to the inviting material of her lace panties. She felt him move his hand around to her bottom, giving it a playful squeeze. Her mouth, warm and wet, paused over his lips, anticipating his next move. He could feel her heat radiating on his legs and wanted desperately to take her right there. She felt his hesitation and pressed her supple lips to his, moving her hand below his waist and placing her palm over his now complete erection, stroking it through his jeans. Not willing to let her gain the upper hand, he shifted his legs so she was forced to spread hers to accommodate his position. His fingers deftly moved between them, and she let out a muffled cry against his mouth when he touched the slick wetness of her swollen lips.

Unbeknownst to the steamy lovers, they had caught the attention of several other passengers. Most of them wished such passionate kisses were in their lives. Little did they know the lust that was threatening to overtake the couple in the shadowed seats behind them.

His fingers pushed inside her as she moved against his hand, barely able to control her appetite. Her face was buried inside his jacket, frantically trying to still her movements so as not to draw unwanted attention. He moved his other hand to her hip to hold her skirt down.

She was attempting to free him from the denim prison with both hands. As soon as her small hand wrapped around his hard cock, he thought he would come up from the seat. With both hands, he grabbed her ass and positioned her to take him. She braced her arm against the seat behind his head and guided him into her. The fiery invasion was a relief to both of them. He pulled her head to his, biting at her lips as her tender opening encased him. The throbbing flesh within her pulsed in time with her own contracting muscles. Trying hopelessly to quell her cries of ecstasy, she kissed him hungrily while grinding her body down onto his. His powerful muscles flexed as he slowly pushed and pulled his manhood inside of her. The friction of his skin on her clit quickened her pulse and pushed her one step closer to the forbidden release.

He pulled her down, willing her to allow him to drive up inside her. He moved his fingers to the pulsating bead buried within her folds and began to work the magic he knew would bring her wanton distress to a close. Their kiss was hot and relentless, acting out the force of passion that they could not. Within moments, she felt a wave that signaled her sublime torture was about to peak.

He felt her tighten around him and wrapped his arms around her, keeping her snug against his body. He continuously moved inside her, a tide ebbing and surging. She tore her mouth from his and buried it in his neck, frantically trying not to scream. Instead, in ragged breath, she whispered his name again and again. His lips sought hers out as he filled her again, his own orgasm brought to speedy head by her intense caresses. Her delicate flesh contracted around him, milking him relentlessly. Swiftly, he shifted, pushing her forward and bracing her against the seat in front of them. His hands dug into her hips, urgently holding her to him. He drove into her, erupting in one fervent moment.

They sat still for several minutes, letting the sounds of the passing city wash over them. Her body was limp in his arms, the blissful sensation still reverberating in her limbs. She slowly woke from the trance that was their lustful exhibition. Their kiss softened to flickering embers of the molten passion that just moments ago had raged. Her hands toyed gently in his short dark hair as she pulled out of the kiss. She opened her eyes to find him once again gazing into hers and smiled a secret smile that only lovers share. He winked back at her and slid her off his lap. Their stop was next, and as they got off, they did not notice the gentleman behind them with the approving grin on his face.

Seduction of Cory

It was a couple of days after Johnny's outrageous dismissal, and I was still seething. Every time I thought about it, I was just sick. No man had ever walked away from Syn. He had to be crazy. What kind of guy walks away from a ready and willing woman? Try as I might, I couldn't get it out of my head. I needed a distraction, and I had one coming up. It wasn't exactly what I wanted, but maybe some much-needed downtime at home would ease my wounded ego. So I headed back to Florida as soon as the shoot wrapped up. On the plane ride, I closed my eyes and thought about some fun in the sun, some margaritas on the beach with my best friend, and some guy-less nights.

Upon arriving home, I immediately called my girl Angela. She said that a group of our friends had made plans to see a local arena football game that night and welcomed me to join them. I jumped at the chance. Maybe a good night of beer drinking and screaming and yelling at a game would relieve some of the aggression I felt toward Johnny. I threw on my favorite pair of jeans, a red T-shirt, and pulled my hair up into a high ponytail. I looked pretty young, so I double-checked my purse for my ID and headed out the door. I felt comfortable and completely at ease when I pulled into the crowded parking lot. I gave Angela a call to find out where they were and began the long trek to the main entrance to the stadium.

Glad I was wearing comfortable shoes, I met up with Angela and a couple of our other friends fifteen minutes later. We were still waiting on several others, so Angela and I took an order for beers and agreed to meet everyone at the seats. We had three minutes until kick off, and Angela and I were struggling to carry our booty back to the clan when I felt a pair of warm arms reach around from behind me and grip the cardboard carrier I was struggling with. I turned to stare into the smokiest pair of brown eyes I'd ever seen. Immediately, my womanly senses kicked into overdrive, and I had to take a deep breath to keep my cool.

I could tell he was saying something, but my mind blocked out the sound while I just stared at his kissable mouth. Finally Angela nudged me out of my trance and introduced me to Cory, brother to our friend Aaron. Handing him the carrier, I smiled, quietly melting inside. He was absolutely adorable. I could tell he was younger, but I didn't know how much. I knew Aaron had a brother, but I didn't know much about him. I was definitely going to find out. So I asked Angela. Nineteen. He was nineteen. My heart sank a little. Oh well. Tonight was supposed to be no guys anyway.

We arrived back just in time for the first play of the game, and as luck would have it, Cory and I sat next to each other. Typical stadium seats, there wasn't much room to spread out, so to make more room, Cory rested his arm behind my seat, and well, what can I say? I just fell into it. We talked for a good portion of the game, missing most of the key plays. I had hardly touched my beer, but I was having a great time. I was disappointed when I looked up at the clock and realized there were only five minutes left in the game. I knew my time with Cory was coming to an end. I couldn't let that happen. I turned to Angela and asked if we had plans for after the game. As the question made its way around to the rest of the group, I sat thinking about what a doll he was. Before I could stop myself, the thought popped into my head: *He'd never walk away from me.*

I couldn't believe it. I was thinking about seducing my good friend's nineteen-year-old brother. I was almost ten years older than him. He was an innocent. All these thoughts raced through my head, but it didn't stop the fact that I wanted him.

The game ended, and we decided to go grab a bite to eat at a late-night burger shop. We could have gone to the moon, and I wouldn't have cared. I was hot for Cory, and if he was going, so was I. I think Angela knew what I was thinking, because she kept giving me these "Don't even think about it" looks. I couldn't help it; he was sexy as hell, with country-boy charm and college-boy good looks. If he was game, then I wanted to play. I knew I had to be subtle in my approach. I wasn't sure what kind of experience he had, if any, and I didn't want to scare him. I wanted to know if he wanted me before I took the dive. My opportunity came unsolicited.

I was getting out of Aaron's truck in the parking lot of the restaurant when Cory reached up to lend me a hand. Impressed by his manners, I accidentally fell into him. My ballet slipper had caught on the running board and was holding me hostage. Cory deftly caught me in his arms as I stumbled out of the truck's hold. As I struggled to straighten myself out, feeling like a complete fool, Cory leaned in close to my ear and whispered, "I knew you'd feel good in my arms." I almost tripped again.

Instead, meeting his gaze, I responded coolly, "But you'd feel much better between my legs."

Surprise flashed in his eyes, but it was subtle. I knew he wasn't a virgin, but he was still innocent. I wanted to change that so badly I could taste it. I walked inside ahead of him, shaking my ass slightly just to tease him a little.

Our late-night feast went on for a little over two hours, finally winding down about 1:00 AM. I was tired from my trip and the long day, but I was hot and stoked at the promise of Cory for dessert. We had flirted all throughout the night, keeping our desire for each other just below simmering so as not to attract the attention of the group. I'm sure Angela knew what I was about, but she was used

to it. I really didn't want Aaron to find out. I wasn't sure how he'd take his little brother being seduced by the girl they called Syn.

We drove back to the stadium to pick up the rest of the cars. I have to give the kid credit. He was sly. Voicing his concern over my safety because I was so tired, he offered to drive me home. Everyone being accustomed to his country kindness, they didn't think anything of it. We got into the car and sped off into the darkness. As soon as the stadium was out of sight, I placed my hand on his muscular thigh and slowly traced my fingers up his leg until I heard him inhale very slowly. I decided to back off, not wanting our evening to end up smoking on the side of the road. He gave me a timid smile, and I placed my hand on his chest and nuzzled my lips against his neck. My breasts were pressed firmly against his arm, feeling his warmth. I whispered quietly in his ear how badly I needed him tonight, and the car swerved slightly. I had to muffle a small giggle as I sat back in the seat. I figured it would be in my best interest to relax until we reached my apartment.

It wasn't long. He drove like a madman back to my place. His eagerness excited me. I was just as eager, but at the same time, there was this little voice in the back of my head. It kept screaming, *He's only nineteen! He's Aaron's little brother!*

I put the voices out of my head as we pulled into the driveway. I checked myself in the mirror as he got out and opened the door for me. Again, I melted—he was just too sweet. Opening the door to my apartment, we walked inside. I didn't bother turning on a light as the moon was nearly full and offered plenty of light for what we'd be doing. I set my keys and pocketbook on the table and slid out of my shoes. He started to say something, but before he could, I crossed to floor to him and put my finger on his lips. When I was sure he wasn't going to speak, I removed my finger and placed my hands on his shoulders. Sliding them up and around his neck, I brought his lips down to mine. I felt his hands go around my waist and pull me closer. Not giving in to his insistence, I continued with the feather light butterfly kisses.

I kept him at bay for several minutes before I opened my mouth fully to him and slipped my tongue inside. His fingers dug into my flesh as he kissed me back, the past hours of innocent flirting transformed into passionate demand. I allowed this young buck to coax my lips into abandoned desire before finally closing off his kiss and moving my kisses down his chin, along his jaw line, to his neck, and back up the other side before coming to rest again on his hungry mouth. His arms were wrapped tightly around my body, holding me against him. I could feel his hard length against my abdomen and sighed in appreciation of what dear Cory had to offer. I slowly pulled out of his strong embrace and took his hand, leading him toward my bedroom. But his stride halted at the couch.

He pulled me back to him and closed his lips around my earlobe. A low grown escaped me, and he laughed softly.

I was at his mercy as much as he was at mine. We drifted into another deep kiss, and he laid me down on the couch, his hand behind my head, and covered my body with his own. My hands raked through his short, spiky hair. His head moved lower down my body, his teeth scraping my erect nipples through my thin T-shirt. My back arched slightly as shockwaves shot deliciously through my body. His hands moved underneath my shirt, pushing it slowly out of the way. His hot touch on my bare skin caused the warmth between my legs to spread, and I opened them around his body. My shirt successfully removed, my breasts now pushed insistently against the satin cups of my bra. A quick glance into my smoldering gaze, and he released them from the fabric barrier. My eyes closed in absolute pleasure as his mouth explored my willing flesh.

Oh, how I wanted him. My seduction wasn't going very well. Here I was, lying beneath him, moaning and sighing like a mewling kitten. He had more skill than I thought. His touch was soft and unhurried, not like I expected, though I wasn't complaining. He was good ... so very, very good. As his mouth moved to my stomach, softly kissing my fevered skin, I pushed myself up on my arms and slowly continued to sit up, subsequently forcing him back. When he was on his knees, I slid off the couch onto the floor in front of him. Taking my cue, he shifted so he was sitting facing me, and my hands began to undo his pants. I was beyond satisfied at young Cory's offering, and without hesitation, I proceeded to show my gratitude. A sharp intake of breath on his part let me know my affection was well received.

After several deep strokes of my soft lips, I could tell he was nearing the end of his rope. Not willing to let our night end so early, I eased off, only to be taken into his grasp and laid back on the coffee table behind me. It was only moments before my jeans were off and my panties pushed aside, allowing his tongue to push into me. My legs were thrown carelessly over his shoulders as his hands playfully toyed with my nipples and his tongue explored every fold of my wet, pulsing womanhood. My hands grasped at him, reaching for anything to pull him deeper into me. I felt his lips close over my clit, and I nearly came off the table. Every nerve ending was on fire, all focused on that one spot where his tongue and lips met to drive me absolutely wild. As he drove me closer and closer to the edge, I begged him to fuck me. Pleading and gasping, I begged for him to fill me.

He hesitated only a second to get his pants off. Still on my back on the coffee table, he pushed my legs back toward my chest and entered me without ceremony. He felt so good I almost came immediately. His strokes were strong and smooth, caressing my most intimate parts. His arms were wrapped tightly around my quivering body,

pressing me into him. His lips moved between my neck and my mouth; his tongue grazed all the skin in between. I whispered his name repeatedly and met his hips with every thrust. We continued this slow dance until I was well into my second orgasm, the first one coming so fiercely I'm sure I blacked out for a moment. Still gasping his name, I clawed at his back as he surged inside me, his own impending explosion imminent. My swollen pussy began to squeeze his throbbing cock as I came again. The coffee table rocked back and forth as he pounded into me, coercing my final frenzied release.

In an almost drunken stupor, I slid off the table onto the floor in front of him and opened my mouth to accept his last thrusts. With my lips and hands enveloping him, he came hard inside my mouth. Watching his face contorted in animal-like ecstasy, I swallowed everything he had to give me. Groaning deeply, he cradled my head in his hands and eased himself slowly out of my wet existence. He brought my mouth up to his and kissed me hard, holding my sweaty, limp body against his.

Eventually, we moved into my bedroom, where I could explore this seduction more thoroughly, but as the night grew longer and the handcuffs tighter, I began to wonder who was seducing whom ...

Freakish Desires

They called him the Freak. It was as much for his out-of-this-world talents in the studio as for his debauched habits in the bedroom. I'd like to say only a select few were allowed knowledge of the latter, ah, but then it wouldn't be quite so wrong. He was not discriminating in his partnerships. He was an equal opportunity sadist. Men held his attentions as much as women, and on more than one occasion, he combined his tastes with an odorous mixture of his drug *du jour*. Never were his paramours quite so shocked as when they discovered the wickedness that lay beneath the façade of the talent extraordinaire.

It was precisely this wickedness that I sought him out for. If ever there was another soul as blackened by circumstance as mine, this freak of a man was in possession of it. I sought to bring him down for two reasons: his sensibilities would not be offended by my dark desires, and when I was successful, I would be doing womankind a service. It was my sordid attempt to redeem a part of myself.

He was a rapist, but not in the traditional sense of the word as most of his partners consented … in the beginning.

He stole their moral innocence, if ever they had one. He took from them their sense of self, their ability to know truth from deceit, and stripped them of their dignity, forcing them to succumb to his dark and twisted desires. He was a puppet master in his theatre of cruelty.

I knew what he was capable of; it was really no different than my own pattern as of late. Only he left his victims breathing, to live with the memory of a night spent so steeped in sexual misdeeds that they might always be scarred. In essence, I think I was a much kinder deviant.

It was purely my own fault that we had not experienced a night together. We had met on several occasions. Each time he made his desires subtly known, and I quietly rebuffed them. The first time my refusal was based on lack of attraction alone. He was not the beefed up piece of meat I had grown accustomed to satisfying my lust with. His presence was dominating in an intellectual sense rather than a physical one. His eyes were dark and his countenance almost feminine. I was unaware of his shadowed behavior. Had I known, I might have taken more of an interest.

By the time I did find out, it wasn't a mere rumor. I heard firsthand accounts. Like bad celebrity gossip, I distanced myself from the freakish happenings so as not to taint my own reputation.

On this night, this mellowed out, moonless misty night, I sought to make my reputation as Syn.

I did not need to dress the part of harlot to attract his attentions. Naturally, he was drawn to my confidence, seeking to dampen my independent spirit. Immediately, he began to circle like a coyote hunting a weak member of the pack.

The atmosphere was heavy, a pulse-pounding beat in my ear and a sweet fog swirling at my feet. The club was full of bright lights and even brighter masses, Day-Glo hair, glitter make-up, and the cheap squeak of vinyl caressing moist thighs. It was an environment I never bothered to indulge in. It was the excess of youth, unintelligence at its finest, sex without skill, blind fucking of random strangers. Of course he would frequent this place, seeking his next willing participant. She would be young, naïve, desperate to please, and feeling special that he chose her. Immediately, her mind would delight in all the empty promises, and she would acquiesce to his request. He would deflower her in a darkened room, in a poorly lit parking space, a needle still in his arm. She would walk away with a lesson learned but always craving his affection one last time.

She would be one of the lucky ones. His time spent on her would be minimized by his need to satisfy an immediate appetite. The ones he chose as pets—those he brought home to participate in his voluptuous misdeeds— they were the ones who suffered. Allowed to think they existed for his eyes alone, he shared and advertised them to his minions. He entertained with the needy, pleading eyes they turned on him. He laughed at their desperation, reveled in their confusion, and when finally after exhausting their mind and bodies he cut them loose, he felt little remorse for the tattered being left crumpled on the floor.

At the present moment, I am unable to either understand or put an end to my craving for their blood. Whether it is a deep-seated need to end the lives of those who bring out the worst in me, or a simple desire to feel mortality literally wash through my hands, I couldn't care less. Though I am not without a higher code, I did seek him out specifically, not to satisfy my lust but to justify his ending by the direct relation of his black heart. Call it trite, call it corrupt justification, I am Syn for a reason. Fuck you if you don't like it.

Soft suede caressed my lithe limbs up to the thigh, in a shade of pink only I would dare. Black satin wrapped around my hips, barely covering my naked ass. Did I care that I was walking sex? No. There would be little opportunity for conversation, and I wanted him to know in no uncertain terms what my purpose was. Glittering magenta covered my unadorned breasts like a second skin, my nipples clearly visible through the supple latex. I wore my hair down, swirling around my shoulders, inviting him to wrap his hands in it and make me scream.

Maybe it was the gaggle of female flesh that migrated toward that corner of the room, maybe it was my keen

sense of the darkness I sought. Either way, it was only a matter of minutes before I located him. I made it a point not to flirt coquettishly but to lock his gaze in a bold invitation. Challenge accepted, I watched in sweet satisfaction as he moved toward me, his attention now focused on my mouth as I licked my lips in anticipation. He was cocky. His crooked smile and the evil glint in his eye were as apparent as the devastated girls he left in his wake.

Upon his approach I simply nodded and offered a neutral smile. He brought my hand to his lips. It was then that I first noticed how utterly kissable those lips were. Soft and sensual, I could imagine them warm and wet, suckling at my most tender parts. I'm sure my clouded gaze didn't go unnoticed. He didn't release my hand but instead brought it down and wrapped his fingers around it. A slight question crossed his face, and I moved into his body, my fingers wrapping tightly in the leather that swathed his lean body. I pulled him close and tight. With my heated breath on his skin, I pressed my mouth to his exposed neck, feeling his pulse, knowing its song was limited. I gave a little moan as his hands found my bare ass and gave a firm squeeze. Mmm, this was going to be fun.

Location was crucial. His place was immediately ruled out, as I couldn't risk leaving behind even a minute trace of myself. I was becoming bored with hotel rooms. It turned out I needn't have worried. As we stepped out into the night, I quickly realized our meeting place was situated in the midst of nothing. Beyond the bright lights and heart thumping beats lay a shallow forest surrounded by fields. We weren't that far outside the city, but I suppose they chose the location for precisely that reason. He began to guide me toward the parking lot, but I stopped. I moved in front of him and spun to face him. Our faces darkened by the shadows, he now looked menacing, and I felt a tiny shiver of fear. Had I believed all the rumors, he would not hesitate to attempt to bring me to my knees if I resisted his charms. This did not concern me much, as long as I wouldn't be the only one in that position.

I stepped closer, resting my hands on his shoulders and my lips just below his ear. I let my touch linger a moment before I whispered a playful request to follow me. He raised a questioning brow, but with his sly smile, he obeyed. His first mistake.

We walked steadily over the grass into the first of the thickening trees. I led him, my cold hand in his warm one, into an area that was peppered with medium-sized trunks and heavy leaves. I couldn't have fashioned a more perfect setting for his delicious demise.

I wanted him on his power trip before I began mine. In fact, I needed it to gain access to him. There was no music here, nothing but earthly silence, a gentle rustle of leaves, and an animal scurrying in the darkness. The only light was that of the marquee from the club, and it only glowed at random through the thick foliage.

We stood facing each other for a moment. I felt very small for a brief second. Then he stepped toward me, and the last moments of his life began.

Even before his lips claimed my own, I tasted him. The sweet, musky scent of his cologne engulfed me. The heady warmth of his body pressing against mine intoxicated me, and even as I languished in his oral caress, I felt the stirrings of my madness, my hunger, and my craving. Itching to taste him, I scraped my nails down his belly, pushing aside the thick material that protected his skin from the chill of the night. Before I had slid my hand inside his pants, he wrenched his mouth from mine and shoved me to my knees. He was in no mood to waste time, but I wasn't about to be rushed. I gave in to his demands only because they suited my own purpose. No sooner did I have his pulsing cock in my mouth did he whip out the little mirror hidden in his coat with a glittering vial. Whatever the white powder was his desire of the moment would only make his death more satisfying.

I glanced up to watch him inhale the substance at the same time I chose to scrape my teeth gently across his taut skin. My reward was a sharply hissed moan and a handful of my hair wrenched in his hand. His action only succeeded in igniting my desire to push the fine line between my pleasure and his pain. So I pushed. I swallowed him deeper, I sucked him harder, and I pressed my sharp nails into his skin as I raked them across his lower back, thighs, and ass. Every time he made a sound, whether agony or appreciation, I stepped it up a little more. In time, a correlation can be made during certain aspects of two different sensations. Soon you will come to associate one with the other, and you will feel dual emotions toward the two separate actions. There was no time for the connection to be permanent, but I was not about to stop.

I continued the assault on his lower extremities as his true freakish desires became overwhelming, and he could no longer be satisfied with the deep welts that had formed over his body. My lips were raw and numb from the chill of the night and the constant abuse of his rigid cock fucking my tender mouth. He attempted to relieve me of my duties, but I remained steadfast in my position. His cries became louder so that I could not tell if he was begging me to stop or continue. I did not take it to heart. I kept going, and he kept showering me with expletives.

Finally, when his desire outweighed his strength, he pushed me violently away from him. It was at this point that I considered the possibility of fucking him. Sucking his throbbing member had me soaked to the core, and my pussy quaked to be filled by something other than my own fingers. I eyed him lasciviously while he attempted to collect himself. His hand raking through his hair, I noticed the stark contrast between his fair skin and the night sky. I marveled at the artistic addition that his blood would make.

After what seemed like ages, he came toward me. Without ceremony, he grabbed the back of my head and kissed me, hard, punishing, and carnal. There was nothing tender in his desire for me. He was in another world, one where I didn't exist, but his pleasure and his pain fought for his attentions. This is where I wanted him. I didn't fight it when he partially quenched my thirst by thrusting his fingers inside me. Both of us on our knees in the cold embrace of the forest, he fucked me with cold hands and even colder eyes. The fire inside me only burned brighter. When enough time had passed, I pulled his hand from inside my dripping folds. Bringing it to my own lips, I suckled each of his fingers. Staring into the empty depths of his soul, I expected to see nothing. I was right.

I stood up and tugged him gently to follow. He stood before me, half naked. I assisted him the rest of the way. It wasn't long before he was completely without clothes or hindering. He was mine; he belonged to the darkness he so lovingly doled out to his victims. Quietly stalking him under the guise of admiring his lean frame, he didn't notice when I slipped his bindings out of the bag that presented itself as an ordinary purse. They were soft so as not to alarm, but they were strong as steel and meant to hold for prolonged torture.

I stood in front of him and slowly stripped away the vinyl that had molded itself to my skin, removing the tiny piece of fabric that had shielded my sex from the rest of the world. The only things left were the suede boots that covered my long, toned legs. I loved the flashy pink, so I left them. It would soften the blow later on.

So there he stood, in all his arrogant glory, the welts on his thighs and ass blazing with heat in the chill of the dark. I was ready to set fire to the rest of him. I pulled him to the closest tree; in his preoccupation with my supple, naked body, he hardly struggled as I bound him to it. It was only after I had finished with the second wrist that he really began to fight. Was it that he discovered the strength of the ties? Or had his intuition crept out from behind the haze of his drugs to send of an alarm bell?

I don't know. I didn't ask. I didn't care.

I was only able to escape the kick of his leg by sheer agility and quick reflexes. I asked him if this was not what he wanted, but he didn't have a reply for me. I moved quickly to the last leg before he changed his mind and started to feign agitation once again. I had him bound but not gagged. I wanted his cries to be heard, his tears absorbed not by some cheap rag but by the earth itself. I wanted his blood to mix with the dampness of his tears and seep into the core to serve as a warning to the rest of hell's angels. Oh, and he was an angel of the darkest sort with the way he played the game and created the role, the hearts he left in his wake and the destruction he cast upon the female sex he so loved and loathed. The blood he shed in the name of love. I looked forward to lighting his way to hell's gates.

As he quieted and waited for my next seduction, I moved back to the bag and drew out my beloved cat-o'-nines. It was braided rope of the highest quality. It shimmered purple in the distant light and cast an almost ethereal glimmer on his pale skin. I lashed him once gently, letting the braids fall in a musical slap on his chest.

He smiled, daring me to go further, and I called his bluff. I lashed again with angry force. The cat sliced through the air and ended with a sting and a hiss from his beautiful lips. I let the sound resonate through the trees. His head thrown back, he did not plead with me, nor did he challenge me. Again, I sliced the whip through the icy air, stinging him again and once more, just to hear his breath fill his lungs. He still did not look at me. I stepped close to him, breathing hotly on his throat even in the dark, taking notice of the pulsing beat just below the tender skin. I pressed my lips to it. His head moved, pressing his lips to my head. It could almost be mistaken for apologetic. But I knew better. Like a kid stealing a cookie, he wasn't sorry he did it—he was just sorry he got caught.

I stepped back, bringing the cat slicing through the air three times in quick succession. This time he cried out. My heart swelled at the sound, and I moved to his backside, to his beautiful, succulent ass. I lashed out at it in defiance. Once, twice, three times, then a fourth. He made no sound. I slid the slender whips down his body, tracing his taut muscles with the heated leather. Meanwhile, my fist reached around to grab his still hard cock and stroke it with the utmost care. Slowly, I let it slide out of my fingers before I cupped his balls, giving them a gentle tug. Beneath that, I let my finger explore the tightened skin and beyond, to that forbidden place that makes most men question their sexuality. Not him. He didn't even allow for a quickened breath when my expert touch pierced his taboo opening. I smiled inwardly, wondering just how far I would take his enjoyment.

Glancing down at the perfectly shaped handle of my cat, I made my decision. Not yet, I decided—I needed to satisfy my own craving first. I circled back around in front of him and pulled his head down to look me in the eye as I lay down on the cold grass and stiff leaves. I slowly spread my thighs, opening my wet entrance. With two fingers, I parted the soft skin that shielded my sex from the elements; with my other hand, I positioned the handle of my cat-o'-nines at the opening of my pussy. Looking him dead in the eye, I guided the supple leather inside me. I watched him salivate as I fucked myself with this object of punishment.

Pushing it as deep as I would allow, I arched as I would against a lover. I toyed with it, generously savoring each inch of it, taunting him. I watched in satisfaction as he began to squirm, his cock protruding unashamed. I caught the tiny diamond at the tip, glistening in the elusive light, and knew it was time. I laid the cat on his chest thrice

more without flinching and finally drew a drop of blood at his collarbone. Immediately, I was upon him. My tongue barely touching his skin, I flicked the harsh liquid into my throat.

I almost laughed at his expression, his eyes wide and astonished. Then I saw the haze settle over him. He began to fight the bindings with the little strength he still had. He did not realize his end was so imminent, but he did understand the next few moments were not about his pain. They were about my pleasure.

With my hand once again lovingly stroking a cock I could have worshipped, I pressed my nakedness against his throbbing back. I could feel each and every rise and fall of the welts I had inflicted against his skin. I caressed the back of his neck with my tongue, and with a shiver, I stepped back. Putting one hand on the place I just kissed, I took my cat in the other and guided it down to his spine to his tight little ass, until I reached that well-hidden hole. Without permission, without care, and with nothing but the saliva from my own mouth, I opened the door to his ruin. His cries falling on deaf ears, I took from him what he delightedly ripped from others. Bound to rough wood in a place where no one dwelled, I emptied him of his will again and again, all the while still stroking the cock he used as a malicious weapon. The lips every woman dreamed of were now the vehicle to express his torture. I pushed the cat and pulled his flesh until he could scream no more, and in the instant I ripped the cat from his body, he spilled his seed and I severed his life.

Walking away wrapped in the supple leather that once adorned him, I glanced back, and in the most artistic fashion did I admire the blood that crawled in heated rivulets down his naked body.

More

M any had come and gone, and there were still many I wanted to try, but he was the one. He was the one I thought of in the quiet; he was the one in my daydreams, in my night dreams, and everywhere but my reality.

I knew that going back was like ripping my heart out. So much had gone down there, and so much had happened since, but there was a pull I couldn't deny. I missed the palm trees, the salt in the air, and the pulse. There was an energy there I didn't find anywhere else. Even at my most miserable, I found inspiration. It was a heart-wrenching separation when I left. It was time to go back to finish what I had started.

My plane landed in the early afternoon, and I knew I had plenty of time before I was supposed to meet my friends for dinner, so I took my time leaving the airport. I watched as families struggled to carry their souvenir-laden luggage to their gates and businesspeople walked while talking on their iPhones and BlackBerries. I sighed contently, knowing I would never again be a tourist in this beautiful city. I would visit other cities for business and pleasure, but here I would be home.

I finally made it to the car. The driver gave me a relieved smile and loaded my carry-on into the trunk. I slid into the dark car and immediately wished I'd asked a friend to pick me up. It was brilliantly sunny out, and the last thing I wanted was to sit in the shadows with another stranger. I shrugged it off as I reconciled myself to the thirty-minute ride to my new home.

As the car hummed along, I closed my eyes and thought of my friends: Erica, whom I hadn't seen in three years but who was like a sister to me; Casey, my hard-partying friend and serial dater; and last but not least, Desiree, the sweetest girl on the planet who had finally found the love of her life. I smiled as I thought of each one of them and the secret they knew. Back in the day, when Orlando was more like my personal playground than anything else, each one of them helped solidify my place in infamy. Erica was my conscience, always warning me against the dangers of my latest antics and the first one with an "I told you so" the next morning. Casey was my partner in crime and always there to be my alibi. Desiree was my antidote; she always knew the right things to say or do when my heart, mind, or body was in tatters.

As misty memories of girls' nights and margaritas wafted through my mind, his image seeped into my thoughts. I immediately remembered back to our first "official"

meeting. I couldn't even recall the last time I blushed, but I did that night. I grinned to myself as I remembered feeling so painfully shy it was like an out-of-body experience. I also remembered the sober punch Erica delivered when she announced to our friends how very "high school" I behaved.

I laughed out loud as that familiar feeling washed over me. It *was* very high school-ish of me. He was a crush of epic proportions, and despite having carved a path miles wide through the male population, I couldn't bring myself to move past it. I sighed again and prayed that he was married with two kids and a dog, or gay with two kids and a dog. I didn't care—anything to put him in the untouchable category.

Oh, but to touch him. Gahhhh, I hated that even four years later I was still hung up on him. It was ridiculous, and I told myself that. Just because I was back in town did not mean things were going to be the same. I had my game plan, and he did not enter into it. No man did. Not even for a night, for a kiss, or for a lingering gaze.

I forced my brain to switch tracks and started a mental to-do list for when I got home. I could start unpacking, but I knew once I got started it would be hard to stop. I decided that I'd only unpack my clothes so I had something to wear tonight and then I'd finish up some paperwork before dinner. I was excited to see my friends. It had been too long.

We pulled up in front of my house, and the driver graciously opened the door for me. I stepped out into the afternoon sunlight and took a breath: humid, grassy, home. I looked up at my new house and smiled. I loved it. I knew I would. It was everything I had wanted. I tipped the driver and grabbed my bag, nearly skipping up the brick pathway to the front door. I dug out the key the realtor had air-shipped to me and opened the door.

Although the large living room was full of boxes, I could see the sunlight filtering over them from the large front windows. Beyond that, I could see the dining room with glass doors that lead out onto the patio. I set my bag down and wandered through the boxes, lightly running my fingers over the labels. In these boxes were remnants of my former life here, mixed with the more recent memories of my life in the Windy City. I wasn't starting over again; I was just beginning a new chapter. I wandered toward the dining room and slid open the patio doors. I could hear the tiny rustle as the resident geckos hurried away from the stranger in their neighborhood. The patio was shaded, but past that the crystal clear pool glittered in full sunlight. Palm trees dotted the landscape, as well as some bold colorful flowers I couldn't name but immediately liked. I added "hire gardener" to my mental to-do list. I walked the length of the patio to the other end of the house and looked inside the family room through the floor-to-ceiling windows and smiled.

My smile faded as I heard my cell phone going off in my purse. *Not a moment of peace,* I thought. I glanced at the caller ID before I answered. It was Erica.

"Hey there!" I said enthusiastically.

"Are you here? Your plane was supposed to land hours ago. Where are you?"

"Calm down, doll. I'm here, and my plane only landed a little while ago. I just got home." I walked back into the house and slowly made my way to the stairs, wondering when my furniture would be arriving.

"Home? You're home already? I thought you were going to call. I would have picked you up."

"I know, but I didn't want you to have to get out of work. So, yes, I'm home and I just realized I have no furniture so let me get off here and give them a call or I'll be crashing on your couch tonight."

"Okay, am I still picking you up tonight? What are you doing for wheels? Are they shipping your car too?" Erica laughed. She thought the idea of me having all my things shipped was ridiculous, but I wasn't packing up my cluttered little condo and driving it all down here myself.

"Yes. Do you have the address? What time are we meeting everyone, and did you guys ever decide where we were going? I have to go car shopping. The Tib was on its last leg, so I figured why try to drive it down here when I was just going to getting a new car anyway?" I slid my shoes off and walked up the stairs, loving the feel of the plush carpeting underneath my feet.

"Do you need me to take you, or did you hire a personal car shopper too?" I knew she was trying to be sarcastic, but I could tell she was a little hurt by my airport snub.

"It would be great if you could take me, thanks. So where are we having dinner again?" I located the master bedroom and was delighted but confused at the sight of my bed in the middle of the room. I sat down on it and scooted back into its familiar comfort.

"Oh, right. Well, we decided for old time's sake to go to Margaritaville. Is that cool?"

I laughed. It was a big tourist place but one of my favorite spots. She knew I was cool with it.

"Sounds good. Well, listen, I've really got to make that call. It seems my bed made it but nothing else. So I'll see you about eight?"

"I'll be there. Later, hun."

"Bye, Erica." I clicked my phone closed and rolled off the bed to go check out my bathroom.

It had a skylight, a large marble counter with two sinks, and a separate shower with a large garden tub. I was in love. Most of the houses up north barely had one window, and I had a whole bathtub surrounded by them. I could live in this bathroom. I really needed to call about that furniture, though, so I turned my attention to getting back downstairs and looking up the number to the moving company.

After about an hour of holding and dialing through menus, I finally located the rest of my furniture and was assured it would be arriving first thing in the morning. I had a bed, I had clothes, and my power and water were on. Things weren't all bad, so Erica's couch was relieved for the night.

I spent the next few hours hanging up clothes, showering, and messing with my hair. I picked out my favorite jeans, a black T-shirt and my "Florida shoes," a casual pair of pale pink sandals that I wore like tennis shoes. I left my hair down for the messy casual look but did my makeup like it was a night on the town. It was a quarter after eight, and Erica still wasn't here. She was the kind of girl who would be late to her own funeral. I smiled to myself, thinking about how this all felt so good and familiar: going out with my friends for a night of music and drinks. I saw headlights flash across the front windows and hurried to dig my wallet out of the carry-on from this afternoon. I slid my ID and credit card into my back pocket and grabbed my Chapstick and keys.

The doorbell rang, and my shoes clicked across the foyer. I turned to glance around at the house, mentally checking door and window locks as I opened the front door. Three big smiles greeted me as Erica, Casey, and Desiree all rushed in for a group hug. We squealed and chattered like high school girls all the way to Margaritaville.

Once inside, I was greeted with more familiar faces as several other friends joined us. We laughed, drank, talked about old times, and made future plans. I lost track of how many Jack and Cokes I had. I'm not even sure I drank a whole one because I kept setting them down to talk to someone or dance. After a while, I figured I must have drank at least two or three because I was really feeling it, so I switched to water. About an hour after the switch, I began to feel a little less light-headed, and we decided to head over the local Perkins for an early/late breakfast.

The festive mood of our party continued on the short ride over and overflowed into the restaurant. I ducked into the ladies room for a minute and was blinded by the harsh fluorescent lighting. After my eyes adjusted, I grimaced at the smeared and frizzy mess staring back at me. Oh, that humidity is a bitch! I wiped at my eyes with a wet paper towel and spritzed some water on my curls to tame down the fuzz. A couple minutes later, I was satisfied that I wouldn't scare people while they ate so I headed back to our crowded table.

Erica had saved me a spot next to her, so I squeezed in, knocking over a water glass in the process. I turned quickly to catch the cascading water with my napkin and was startled by a familiar smile and the brightest pair of steel-blue eyes I'd ever seen.

Ryan. The name caught in my throat as I struggled to get the water and remain conscious. In one cool motion, he took the napkin from my hand, caught the water

before it hit his lap, and extended his other arm in a hug. I entered the friendly embrace and was immediately thrown back three years ago to the last time I was so close to this man. His scent, his warmth—it all was so achingly familiar.

"Hey there, stranger," he whispered in my ear. I pulled back to look at him. He was smiling. I smiled back.

"Hey, there. I didn't expect to see you here." I sat back down in my chair and began to fidget with the silverware.

"I heard you were back and figured you weren't going to come find me, so I'd have to come to you."

I nearly fell out of my chair. What was this? I gathered my thoughts about me and responded.

"I didn't know you'd want to be found. I would have bet you were settled with two point three kids and a white picket fence."

I knew that wasn't the case, though. Desiree had done a pretty good job of filling me in on the comings and goings of Mr. Ryan Edwards.

I noticed the slight turn of his body toward me, and I looked up at him.

"Nope, just doing my best to get over the girl who tried to break my heart."

I nearly choked on the air in my lungs. I had no response. I just stared blankly at him, looking for some sign that he didn't just say what I thought he'd just said. It was then that Erica elbowed me in the ribs, and I jerked toward her. I noticed the waitress standing there, watching me impatiently.

"Oh, um, another water and, umm, scrambled eggs with wheat toast, please." I looked back at Ryan and he was talking to a guy I didn't recognize next to him. I turned to Erica and told her I was going to get some air and I'd be right back. She asked if I was okay, and I nodded as I walked away.

Once outside, I still felt stifled. *Broke his heart? He was talking about me, right? Why would he say that if he wasn't? But how did I break his heart? Last I checked, he'd barely known I was alive. Arrrrgh!!!*

I didn't want to get into this. I didn't want to get wrapped up in guy drama. That part of my life was over. I was here because I missed Florida and my friends, not because I wanted to pick up where I left off.

Outside in the heavy night air, I began to relax. I didn't have to get involved in anything I didn't want to. It was the excitement of the night that was making me so static. I took a few deep breaths and pushed Ryan's words out of my head. I was about to walk back inside when someone spoke up behind me.

"So you came back."

I nearly jumped at the sound of his voice. I should have known. Where one was, the other was sure to follow. I turned my head slowly, hoping I was hallucinating.

"Hi, Jack."

He gave me a tense smile and stepped closer.

"Des mentioned you were moving back. I didn't think you'd have the guts."

I see I was going to pick up *exactly* where I left off.

"Do we have to start here, Jack? It's been years. Things change, I've changed. I'm not interested in the games anymore." I took a step in the direction of the door. I wanted to get away from him. I didn't want to remember this part.

"But you're still interested in him, aren't you? Some things never change, and I'm willing to bet that if you're still carrying the torch for him, you won't be able to stay away from me. "

His look was challenging but hesitant.

My back to him, I turned my head and stated, "He said I broke his heart."

I heard the sharp intake of breath, and my fears were confirmed. *He knew.* My thoughts started racing. *What did this mean? Did he know before or after we started sleeping together?*

"He said that to you? Tonight? He's such a fool. I tried to show him you weren't good enough, but he kept insisting there was something between you two."

Tears started to well up in my eyes. Slowly, the scene played in my mind. I remembered the night everything unfolded. We were all at Pleasure Island, dancing, drinking, and having a great time. The evening was coming to a close, and we all headed back to Ryan and Jack's place for a more private after party. I remember thinking that it would be a great opportunity to ask Ryan out, but after a couple more drinks, I couldn't remember my name, much less my agenda. The next thing I knew, I was waking up in Jack's bed.

I sneaked out of the condo, noticing as I left Ryan tangled up in his ex-girlfriend's arms on the couch. My heart sank, and several days later, Jack and I continued our physical relationship. I never stopped crushing on Ryan, but I wasn't about to torture myself by hanging around him, so I distanced myself from that particular scene. Although Jack looked a lot like, acted similar to, and was like a brother to Ryan, I had no feelings for him. He was the closest thing I could get to Ryan so I took it.

Our relationship lasted for about six months before Jack announced he was engaged to his long-term girlfriend. I felt no remorse, no sorrow, only longing. So I left, and I didn't look back for three years.

I turned around to face Jack. "You son of a bitch. You set it up. You planned the whole thing to keep me away from him." Tears threatened to spill down my cheeks, and I swallowed hard.

He walked toward me, stopping inches away. "You don't belong with him. End of story."

"It's not up to you, Jack." One tear escaped, and I quickly brushed it away with the back of my hand.

"I made it up to me. He's too good for girl like you."

I couldn't hold back the tears now as, one by one, the possibilities with Ryan drifted away with the tears. "You didn't know me then, and you sure as hell don't know me now. I'm done with this shit."

I held my head up, my eyes glistening by the light of the restaurant sign, and walked determinedly toward the darkness of the parking lot. Realizing I didn't have a car here, I kept going till I hit the street and flagged down a taxi.

I gave the driver my address through quiet sobs and closed my eyes. This shouldn't matter so much, but I knew telling myself that wouldn't do any good. It did matter. It mattered that Ryan was the only guy during that chaotic time in my life I actually felt something genuine for. It mattered that Jack played not only me, but Ryan too. It mattered that my heart hurt thinking about Ryan's broken heart. *He must know I had been sleeping with Jack.* A fresh wave of tears erupted at this thought, and I quit trying to keep up. I let them slide down my face, eventually pooling in the hollow of my neck.

The taxi slowly pulled up in front of my house, and I gave him what was left of the cash I'd taken out of the ATM earlier that night. I thanked him quietly and walked up the stone path to my front porch. I had forgotten to turn the light on and was a little startled at how dark my street was. I fidgeted in my pockets for my house keys and only came up with my phone and some change.

Shit! I thought. I had left my keys on the table at the restaurant. As I began to call Erica, I saw a movement on the porch and instantly stopped.

"Forget something?" Ryan. He was here. With my keys.

"You left without saying good-bye." His tone was accusatory but playful. Immediately, I thought of my tear-stained face and hoped it was dark enough for him not to notice. He stepped onto the path, dangling my keys.

I couldn't think of anything to say so I just took the keys and walked past him to the porch. He quickly came up behind me and put his hand over mine as I tried to unlock the door. A moment later, we stood in the living room staring at each other, boxes and furniture piled haphazardly around us. The house was mostly dark, with only the lights from the street filtering in and making awkward shadows around us.

I didn't know what to say. Hours ago, I was having the time of my life reconnecting with old friends. I didn't know I was going to step directly back into my old life. I was tired and not up to dealing with old drama, but just as I made up my mind to tell him, he spoke: "I know you were sleeping with Jack. I just don't know why."

His voice startled me, but his words drilled a hole to the center of my heart. It hadn't mattered before if he found out. The damage had been done, but now that he was standing here in front of me, and I knew we were on the precipice of something, it was the last thing I wanted to hear.

"I can't really tell you myself. It happened once, and there never seemed a good reason to stop."

"His girlfriend might have thought different."

I hoped he couldn't see the shame on my face.

"I didn't know about Erin until it was too late." It was a lame excuse, but it was all I had.

"Too late? It's not like driving over a cliff." I couldn't tell if he was angry or trying to be funny. His voice was an emotionless mask.

"I made a mistake. No, I made several years of mistakes. I never said I was perfect. I never tried to be. I am me, or I was me. Listen, I was a different person then. I was working through a lot of things, and I was very confused."

"You never seemed confused when we talked. You certainly didn't seem confused when you were sleeping with my best friend."

"No, you're right. I wasn't confused about you. I knew how I felt, but I also knew how I must look to you. Once I'd been with Jack, I figured any remote chance I might have had with you was out the window. So what was the point?"

He moved through the shadows between the boxes, closer to me. My breath quickened as his warmth sent chills down my spine. He lifted his hand to my cheek. When I turned away from it, he caught my face in his other hand. He looked me squarely in the face.

"What I saw was a girl I really liked struggling to get it together. What I saw was a woman I was trying to get to know better but who kept disconnecting from me."

I didn't want to think what he was saying was true. If it was, I was not only a blind fool, but I'd also spent much wasted time longing for something I could have had long ago.

"Why didn't you tell me?"

He laughed.

"Why didn't I tell you? Why didn't you tell me? I spent a year forcing conversations about football with you just to find out after you left that you liked me. I felt like a high school kid."

I stepped back and pulled in a deep breath and then sighed.

"All this time."

He looked at me as if he were going to say something but thought better of it. He turned around to stare out the window. "What now?" he asked.

I thought before I answered. What could there be between us now? I had promised I hadn't come back to get involved with anyone. I had work to do, a new life that I liked and wanted to continue, and I couldn't afford to be sidelined by drama.

"Nothing. There is nothing now. What we had is past. We can't go back, and that whole thing with Jack has just shadowed things."

"Listen, I don't care about Jack. I know why he did what he did, and for all purposes, it worked. But we're adults, and we can make our own decisions. I think you at least owe me a chance to get to know that girl I met four years ago."

I wanted to say yes so bad, but I couldn't. I knew there was too much history in the way. We would always be staring in the face of my past.

He came up beside me and spoke again. "What if I told you I wasn't going to let you say no?"

My head whipped around to face him. I didn't have a response to that. He put his arms around me and pulled me close to him.

"I think you have really made poor decisions concerning both of us, and maybe it's time I made some decisions. I think you owe me."

I looked up into his wide blue eyes, looking for the joke behind his words, but I found nothing but intense sincerity. I wanted this so bad I could taste it, but I couldn't be sure what he was offering. I'd never let another guy make decisions for me. I was always in control. My mom once referred to me as a freight train in relationships. I just ran over everything, not caring what or who got in my way. I guess Ryan had already been a casualty. Why on earth would he come back for more?

As if he were reading my mind, he said, "I've never thought about another girl like I've thought about you.

I think it's time to get you out of my head and into my reality."

Every other thought I had simply fell out of my head, and for the first time I let myself think we could do this. I felt a slow warmth slip and slide through my body. It was familiar yet strange. It wasn't a sexual response but something else, something more.

"Okay. We can try this, but I can't make any promises. I suck at relationships."

He laughed again, and I melted a little at the sight of his easy smile.

"We can't always be good at everything, and from what I hear, you've just about got everything else covered." I gazed at him incredulously, not believing what he just said. My expression finally registered with him, and he began stammering.

"No, that's not what I meant. I mean I heard you're good at a lot of things. No, that's not right. I mean. Okay, Erica said your business was doing well and that your novels were selling. That's all I meant. I swear." He looked as though he was about to break a sweat, and then it was my turn to laugh.

"It's okay, and things are going really well. You asked Erica about me?"

"Well, I never really had to. She always offered the information." I smiled, remembering Desiree's oh-so-subtle ways of filling me in on Ryan's news.

"I know the feeling."

We stood there for a while, just holding onto one another in the streetlight spilling into my cluttered living room. I was the first to speak.

"I really should get to bed. They are bringing the rest of my furniture first thing in the morning."

His arms tightened around me, and I smiled inside.

"You have somewhere to sleep?"

Not wanting to set him on another fumbling explanation, I quickly answered. "They managed to deliver my bed and all my boxes, so yeah, if I can find the sheets I have a somewhere to sleep."

"Need me to help?"

I didn't really look forward to him leaving, but I knew the sheets were upstairs in one of the boxes in the spare bedroom, and I didn't think he and I getting that close to my bed was such a good idea tonight.

"Thank you, but I know where they are. It will only take me a few minutes."

"Do you have plans tomorrow?"

A giddy laugh bubbled up inside me, and I fought to suppress it. I felt like a teenager. "I'll be unpacking, and then Erica is taking me to get a new car."

He laughed and released me from his arms. I was immediately sad. I liked it there.

"Two girls on a car lot. That should be interesting."

I playfully punched him in the arm. "Hey, I know my way around cars. Don't worry about me."

"Oh, I'm not worried about you. I worry about the salesman." We both laughed as we walked toward the door. He stepped across the threshold into the humid night air and turned toward me. His voice low, he bent to my ear and said, "I want to kiss you so bad I can taste it, but I know I won't be able to stop. Not tonight."

I couldn't move, couldn't breathe. My breath was caught in my throat as his misty whispers in my ear continued, "I want more from you. More than I've ever wanted from someone."

I took a step back from him and looked at his face. More? More than sex? What's more than that? Then it hit me what he was looking for, and my legs nearly gave out. I'd never had such an exchange with a guy. I'd always been very adept at reading guys because usually they always wanted pretty much the same things, just in different orders. Ryan wasn't interested in the typical menu, but I wasn't sure I could deliver.

I gave him another hug and told him to call me. I closed and locked the door behind me. My mind was so tired, yet it was replaying the conversation over and over again. I wanted to run and call Erica, but at the same time I didn't believe it was true. Only in movies did the girl finally get the guy.

I went to bed with a lot on my mind that night and woke up with even more. I wasn't wondering if it had been true anymore but whether or not it was going to continue.

It was 8:00 AM when the doorbell rang, and I figured it was either Erica wondering what happened to me last night or the movers with the rest of my life.

It was neither. It was Ryan with several plastic bags.

"I didn't think you had time to stock the fridge yesterday so I took the liberty of getting a few things to keep you going during your unpacking."

I wanted to kiss him, but I refrained. Instead I took stock of my just-out-bed appearance and hoped he wouldn't notice the disheveled ponytail piled on top of my head, the ratty T-shirt I'd had for seventeen years, and the barely there cotton shorts.

"That's really sweet of you. I thought you had something going on today."

"No, you told me to call you, but I never said I had anything going on. I thought I'd come by and help. If that's okay?"

Okay? Of course it was okay. I turned my head so he couldn't see the mile-wide smile plastered on my face. I wanted to scream.

"They should be here soon, so I'm going to run upstairs and change real quick." I was never so self-conscious of my bralessness than I was at that very moment. I wanted nothing more than to throw him down and take him on my kitchen floor, but I wanted to do this right.

"You look fine to me, but I might get mad if the moving guys start checking out your ass in those shorts."

I blushed, secretly thrilled that he noticed, but I raced upstairs to find a pair of jeans and a bra. I fixed my ponytail a bit and was brushing my teeth when I heard footsteps behind me.

"So what's with grocery delivery boy downstairs?" I nearly choked on my toothbrush as Erica's head popped up in the mirror behind me.

"Oh. Ryan. Yeah. He brought me my house keys last night."

"Did he open the doors too?"

I groaned at her poor attempt at sexual innuendo. "No, he didn't even stay the night. We talked. He left and came back to help this morning." Saying it like that sounded so lackluster. It didn't do justice to the butterflies in my stomach.

She scooted up onto the counter between the dual sinks.

"So what's going on? I was pretty shocked to see Jack walk in right after you left. Did you talk to him?"

"Yeah, we exchanged some words. I'm not worried about Jack. He's a dick, and I'm not going back there with him."

Erica picked up a new tube of lipstick and twisted it up and down.

"Well, he may be a dick, but he is your new boyfriend's best friend."

I looked at her, not sure what to say. I hadn't thought about Jack and Ryan's friendship. I didn't really know

what to think about it. Ryan knew about Jack and me, so obviously something had been worked out if he was still friends with him and wanted to be with me. I don't know. I didn't want to think about that. I just wanted to continue this giddy bubbly feeling. I flashed a cheesy grin at Erica.

"He's not my new boyfriend yet. I don't know exactly where we are, but it's a start and I'm not going to let Jack ruin it. Come on, let's go downstairs."

We changed the subject to the day's agenda and agreed to leave for the dealerships at 2:00 PM no matter how far along we had gotten with the unpacking.

While we were upstairs, the movers had arrived, so Ryan and Desiree, who had come with Erica, had taken charge of directing them to various rooms. While my house slowly filled up with my furniture, Erica and I started moving boxes from the living and dining rooms to their proper places. Once everything was inside, it was nearly two, so we called it quits.

Erica was going to run Desiree home because she had to work, and I was going to grab a quick shower. I waited for my friends to leave before I turned to Ryan. He also had to work that night, and I knew he was ready to hit the showers too.

"Thank you for all your help today. You guys really gave me a head start on the unpacking."

He came up and pulled me into his arms.

"I was glad to help. I wish I could stay and help you get through these boxes."

"Don't worry about it. I'm going car shopping anyway. I can't depend on Erica forever. Are you working tomorrow?" My fingers drifted lazily over his neck and shoulders.

"Anxious to put me back to work?" He laughed the laugh I was quickly growing to adore.

"Well, that would be a help, but I was thinking more about something I think we need to talk about before this can go any further."

He stepped back and his face instantly changed from relaxed to concern.

"Jack," he said. His answer wasn't a questions so much as it was a statement. He knew as well as I did that we needed to work through that if we stood any kind of chance.

Reluctantly, I agreed.

"We can't ignore it, and I need to know how this is going to haunt me." I saw a flash of anger cross his face before he recomposed his concerned expression. He pulled me back to him and rested on the stool at the kitchen counter.

"It isn't going to haunt you. Jack messed up. We worked it out. He's still my best friend, but he's not going to get involved anymore."

I gave him a skeptical look.

"Believe it or not, there are guys out there who can resist you."

I gave a little shocked gasp before I realized he was teasing.

"I wasn't insinuating that he would try to come between us like that again. I'm worried that if you and I can actually make this work, at some point Jack and I are going to interact. I don't want you to always be wondering if we're sleeping together."

"That's a legitimate question. I can't say that the thought isn't going to cross my mind at some point, but I'm giving both of you the benefit of the doubt. Maybe that's stupid on my part, but he's my best friend and you're my girl, and you two aren't exactly pals these days, so I really don't think I have anything to worry about."

"You're right about us not being pals. I just don't want it to be weird."

"I'm not worried about it. Jack and I don't hang out a lot anymore. We work together, and he does his thing and I do mine. He's got Michelle, and now I've got you. You worry about me, not Jack. I'll handle Jack."

"Worry about you? What am I worrying about you for?" He leaned in close and softly kissed the hollow of my throat.

"Worry about me devouring you right this minute if I don't get out of here." I gave a little laugh and pushed out of his arms.

"Well, then, by all means go."

He got up off the stool and walked to the door, no longer having to sidestep boxes and stray chairs.

"I'm going, but I will be back. Same time tomorrow?"

I gave him a hug and walked down the stone path.

"Won't you be tired from work?" I said.

"Okay, how about 10:00 AM then?"

"I'll be here."

And I was, and so was he. For three weeks we put my house in order, went to our respective jobs, and lived our lives in orbit of each other. I was going crazy. I wanted him so badly I was afraid I might have to take stock in Energizer batteries. We talked, we cuddled, we kissed, but we always pulled back before we crossed that line.

I had hoped he was in as much agony as I was, but he never seemed to show it. He was always so calm while I was left in a panting pool of desire. We planned a dinner party with some friends for the night of our one-month anniversary. Neither of us had actually mentioned the word anniversary, but we both knew it. My house was finally complete. I had decided at the last minute to do some redecorating, and yesterday the final touches had been delivered. I was excited to show off my new home.

We invited Erica and her boyfriend, Will, Desiree and her fiancé, and Casey and her man du jour, along with some friends of Ryan's and their dates. It was set to be a great evening. Good food, good friends, and good conversation.

Everything was set to start at seven, so at six thirty I was upstairs putting the finishing touches on my makeup while Ryan was doing the same to the appetizers in the

kitchen. I had just finished putting on my stockings when he came up behind me and slid his arms around under my breasts. His lips nestled in that ultrasensitive part of my neck, and I ducked to get away. His arms tightened, and he proceeded to kiss me despite my protests. Finally, I wrestled out of his embrace enough to turn around and face him.

I wasn't expecting the look I encountered in my about face. It was something that bordered on anger and pain. Immediately, I asked him what was wrong. His answer was simple: "I need you."

I felt like a cartoon caught in a "huh?" moment. My jaw dropped open, and I was speechless.

He put his hand over my heart and spoke again. "I got what I wanted, now I want what I need."

A delirious little laugh threatened to erupt, but I closed my mouth tightly until it passed. Calmly, I looked him square in the eye, and with every ounce of self-control I possessed, I said to him, "In four hours you can have anything you want, but for now you are serving dinner."

With that, I turned and practically ran downstairs before I changed my mind. I'd waited so long for this that there was no way I was going to succumb with only half an hour to satiate years and weeks of wanting this man.

The doorbell rang a little after seven, and Ryan descended the stairs looking completely composed to answer it. Our friends trickled in over the next half hour, and everyone settled into comfortable conversation. Drinks and appetizers were served, and dinner was met with high compliments to the chef. The evening played like a movie on low in the background. I only had eyes for Ryan that evening. Every so often, he would catch my eye, and I'd blush all the way down to my toes. He didn't have to say a word; the look in his eyes told me what was going through his mind. The fact that we kept our hands to ourselves the entire evening just made matters worse. I never thought my fingers could actually ache from not touching someone, but they did. I felt like I was being starved. I kept thinking back to our very first conversations four years ago. I remembered how nice he was, how interested he seemed, and how futile my hopes were. My mind occupied, I made polite conversation with our friends and even attempted to entertain with stories from my stint in the cornfields of Indiana.

Eventually, the evening began to wind down, and one by one, our couples left. Ryan walked the last pair to the door, and I picked up some glasses and walked them into the kitchen. As soon as the door clicked, silence deafened the house. I stood very still, not sure what to do. I had waited so long for this, and now the girl who wrote erotica for a living didn't know what to do. How ironic.

I heard him walk across the foyer until he reached the carpet. When I didn't hear anything more, I turned around and saw him standing in front of the windows. I gazed at him. From the top of his spiky blond hair to the bottom of

his dress pants, I was head over heels for him. Neither of us moved for what seemed like an eternity. Finally, he said my name. It hung in the air like the moisture after a hard rain.

I walked over to him, and he took my hand. Without meeting my eyes, he brought my hand to his lips and turned it over to kiss my palm. Tiny shocks crawled up my arm then down my spine to my stomach, where they met with the butterflies that had taken up permanent residence since Ryan had become a part of my life. I sighed as he continued kissing me: my wrist, the inside of my elbow, my shoulder. By the time he reached my collarbone, my breaths were staggered and my legs could barely hold me up. He sensed my weakness and sank down onto the couch, pulling me down with him.

Barely a glance had passed between us before our lips met. It was a kiss to end all kisses. Soft, unyielding, demanding, and sweet, it was a preview of what was to follow. His fingers tangled in my hair as he pressed my body back into the cushions. My fingers deftly worked at the buttons of his shirt, exposing inch after inch of sun-bronzed skin and tousled hair. Once I made contact with skin, I felt his sharp intake of breath and teased him by lightly raking my nails across his hardened nipples. His body surged toward mine, and our kiss deepened.

His hand ran up my leg to the top of my thigh, where he played with the lace of my stocking and now it was my turn to react to the touch of skin on skin. I arched my back, shoving my breasts toward him. I ached to get out of my clothes, to get him out of his. I craved to feel his touch everywhere. He must have had the same idea, because the next move was his hand sliding behind my back and easing down the zipper of my dress. He pulled back and knelt between my legs as he eased the black silk down over the top of my arms and over my breasts until it reached my waist. His eyes never left mine, and even though he was taking his time exposing the length of my body, I felt warm from the inside out. Once he had my dress completely off, he covered my scantily clad body with his own, and I nearly jolted off the couch from the full skin-on-skin contact. He was hard-bodied and I was soft and supple, yet somehow the combination created something so delicious the only thought I could form was *more.* I knew then I would never be able to get enough of him.

I shoved myself up toward him and caressed his lips before tracing down his jaw line to the side of his neck, where I nibbled gently. A small growl gurgled in his throat as I did this, and I smiled. I continued with my seductive kisses until I'd made it to the base of his throat, where he decided he'd had enough and brought his mouth down on top of mine. Coaxing my tongue into his mouth, he distracted me with his teasing kisses as he slid his hands inside the cups of my bra and moved the tight lace to reveal my taut, rosy nipples. His gentle touch sent electric shocks through every nerve, causing me to cry out a little against his mouth. Quickly, he moved his mouth down and covered my breast, tasting me,

teasing me. When I thought I might lose it, he moved over to the other one and started all over again. With just this simple touch, I was writhing beneath him, silently begging him not to stop. The butterflies had turned to hot, white liquid in my stomach, surging with every lick and suck of his mouth. My hands were restless, moving from his back to his shoulders, to his arms, and over again. Just when I thought I couldn't stand it anymore I forced myself to be still and shoved against him, forcing him back against the couch in a sitting position.

I quickly took advantage of his surprise and straddled him, pressing my breasts against his bare chest and my lips against his. His strong arms wrapped around me in an instant and pulled me even deeper into his mouth. In this position, I was very aware of his hardened member against my thigh and another wave of pleasure bubbled up inside me. I slowly began moving my hips against him. He groaned and tightened his arms around him in an attempt to stop me. When I didn't, he changed tactics and slid one hand to my smooth bare ass and the other to the slippery wetness between my legs. I gasped loudly and buried my mouth in his neck as his fingers found the throbbing nub that made my whole body convulse. He worked it like a pro until my chest was heaving and I was struggling against him.

I lifted my head to look at him, and the hungry gaze caught me off guard. He shifted his legs and forced me to straddle him wider. Before I realized what he was doing, I was leaning back with his hand supporting my back while he slid two fingers inside me and dipped his head to tease my swollen breasts. I could feel the heat welling up inside me, threatening to overflow, but I didn't fight it. I let it overtake me until I was only a gasping, shaking pool of ecstasy.

I slowly righted my body and rested my head on his chest. Only a few moments passed before I slid off his body and onto the floor between his knees. Looking up at him with the doe-eyed gaze I'd perfected many times over, I quickly unzipped his pants and released the throbbing mass underneath. The heat radiating from him made my mouth water, and I wasted no time sliding him past my lips down my throat. A loud groan emanated from him, and he shivered. I continued working my tongue, lips, and fingers around his thickly veined shaft until I tasted the salty liquid subtly seeping from the tip. A few tender flicks of my tongue across the top and he was suddenly on the floor, poised above me in one swift motion.

My legs were quivering, waiting for the culmination of all this waiting. He leaned down and gently caressed just below my ear.

"I want more."

I turned my head slightly, touching my lips to his. I gently lifted my hips as he surged within me, and I gave him everything I had.

Printed in the United States
by Baker & Taylor Publisher Services